KU-467-263

The Yarns of Sid Seven-Legs

Alan J Hill

The Book Guild Ltd

First published in Great Britain in 2022 by
The Book Guild Ltd
Unit E2 Airfield Business Park,
Harrison Road, Market Harborough,
Leicestershire. LE16 7UL
Tel: 0116 2792299
www.bookguild.co.uk
Email: info@bookguild.co.uk
Twitter: @bookguild

Copyright © 2022 Alan J Hill

The right of Alan J Hill to be identified as the author of this
work has been asserted by them in accordance with the
Copyright, Design and Patents Act 1988.

All rights reserved. No part of this publication may be
reproduced, transmitted, or stored in a retrieval system, in any form or by any means,
without permission in writing from the publisher, nor be otherwise circulated in
any form of binding or cover other than that in which it is published and without
a similar condition being imposed on the subsequent purchaser.

This work is entirely fictitious and bears no resemblance to any persons living or dead.

Typeset in 11pt Minion Pro

Printed on FSC accredited paper
Printed and bound in Great Britain by 4edge Limited

ISBN 978 1914471 773

British Library Cataloguing in Publication Data.
A catalogue record for this book is available from the British Library.

For Brooke and Phoebe

And for all grandparents who like to read to their grandchildren!

DUNDEE CITY COUNCIL

LOCATION
CENTRAL CHILDREN'S

ACCESSION NUMBER
CO1 075 271X

SUPPLIER	PRICE
A&x	£7 99
CLASS No.	DATE 23/6/22

CHAPTER 1

WHAT DO I DO NOW?

Sid's life hung by a thread. But that was OK because Sid's life regularly hung by a thread. So, nothing to worry about here, except this time, Sid's life really did hang by a thread. That is a lot of hanging from threads. Sid was a common garden variety English spider. His real name was 'Argiope aurantia', but his friends called him Sid, so that is what we will call him.

Sid is on the end of his single piece of thread, hovering over a toilet as the little girl screams at him, at her mum, at her dad, and from the volume of the screams, everyone in the county of Dorset.

"*Spider!*" screamed Lizzie.

Sid thought, *what do I do now?* while at the same time ducking as the slightly damp (urggh) toilet brush swished past him. Now you might be wondering what a garden spider is doing in a house hovering over a toilet when it should be outside spinning a web amongst the bushes and trees of Lizzie's back garden. To explain, we have to firstly go back to when Sid was born and then back to a few days ago when he lost his only remaining sister, Jayne. Jayne had eight legs, so she was known as... Jayne.

So, the day that Sid was born...

Garden spiders live for any time between one year and several years, and Sid's mum laid her eggs in the autumn. That is what mum spiders do in the autumn – they lay eggs and then put them in a big web sac to protect them from other predators. Crows really like spider eggs as a starter, followed by a main course of worms and a nice juicy crane fly larva for pudding. These are called leather jackets. I know it is a strange name, but it's because they look like John Travolta in *Grease*.

Anyway, these spider sacs can have hundreds of eggs in them, and on the spring day that Sid was born, there was him and 157 brothers and sisters crammed into the sac. The spiderlings, which is the name for baby spiders, hatch from their own eggs but stay in the sac through the winter. It was that busy in there it was like the queue for the Tidal Wave at Thorpe Park. The sac started to split and before you could say, 'look, there's a lot of spiders', there was indeed a lot of spiders.

Spiderlings are amazingly fast, and their skin is almost see-through when they come from the sac, but they are quicker than skates on ice, and when the sac breaks open, they scatter outwards as quickly as ripples in a pond. But this was going to be a bad day for Spider Mum and especially for all Sid's 157 brothers and sisters.

Big Eddie was the boy who lived next door to Lizzie. He smelled funny and was always calling her and her friends names like Soft Face and Dippo. He was called Big Eddie because he was big, and his name was Eddie. His mum said he had big bones, but Lizzie thought most of the bones must be in his tummy if that was the case. He was just a twelve-year-old boy with a seven-year-old girl as his neighbour. Oil and water.

He was in the old oak tree that overhung Lizzie's garden when Sid's sac split and him and his family made a break for life. Shouting something like 'here's Eddie', Big Eddie jumped from the oak, landing with his size five adult boots (I told you he was big) directly on top of Sid and all of his brothers and sisters. Cruel boy. Luckily for you, me and the story, two spiders managed to get out of the sac just before Eddie landed.

Yes, you are right. It was Sid and Jayne, but this is the point in his life when Sid stopped being Sid and became Sid Seven-Legs. Big Eddie killed 156 spiderlings in one jump and took off Sid's eighth leg at the same time. The spiderlings were gone in a second, and it had taken Spider Mum five weeks to name them all. But like all spider mums, she had not waited for the birth; she had moved on. Some said she left to find herself, but I guess we will never know.

Jayne helped her brother and dragged him under a rhododendron so that they could not be seen by Big Eddie who was now leaping around like a cross between SpongeBob and a lower division centre forward playing for a club threatened with relegation. Lizzie saw all this from her bedroom window and shouted downstairs to her mum, "Big Eddie's in our garden again, Mum. Shall I tell him to get out?" She was too late, though, as Eddie, damage to the spiderlings already done, was scrambling back over the fence into his own version of the world that did not include little girls, skipping, holding hands or cabbage patch dolls. Under the leaves of the rhododendron, Sid and Jayne hugged each other and held hands and hands and hands.

You see not many people know this, but I will let you in on a secret. Although it looks to you and me that a spiderling has eight legs, it uses three of them as arms and hands and five of them as legs. Nevertheless, this was the moment when eight became seven.

Jayne was panting and said to Sid, "What happened, Sid? One minute the sac was splitting, and all the light came in, and then the next thing everything is dark, and everyone's gone?"

Sid was Jayne's older brother as his egg had hatched four days before his sister's in the sac, so he knew it was his job to protect her. He said, "It was something to do with that young human who was climbing the fence, Jayne. Look to where the sac was." He pointed and all that was there was a deeply imprinted size five bootprint in the soft, peaty mud. Every one of their brothers and sisters were gone. Splattered, to be quite accurate, but at least they did not suffer.

"What's happened to your leg, Sid?" asked Jayne.

"It's only a flesh wound," replied the brave spiderling.

"Well, it's that much flesh it made up a whole leg," said Jayne. "Sid, you only have seven legs. From now on, you must be known as Sid Seven-Legs." And of course, he was.

The brother and sister then developed the closest bond two sibling spiderlings had ever had; after all, they were the only two surviving members of the 158 in their sac. So, later on that year, in the summer, when Jayne went missing, Sid just did not know what to do!

CHAPTER 2

SPIDER TALK!

We now move through time. It is three months or more since Sid and Jayne came out of the sac, and they did something that is really unusual for brothers and sisters. They became best friends. They both set up separate homes in the hedge at the end of Lizzie's garden, but their homes, actually webs, were only a branch apart, hidden amongst the leaves.

Many people are frightened of garden spiders, but they are quite beautiful and are also known as orb-weavers because their webs are orb-shaped. Even spiderlings have the ability to weave intricate, delicate webs all by themselves without any help from Spider Mum. Sid and Jayne had each other and were always helping each other out with their new web designs and became spiderling experts who, after three months, became fully grown spiders who were experts in web design. The hedge at the end of their garden was their entire world, and within this, Sid and Jayne became authorities in their version of the World Wide Web or WWW for short.

Many of the other spiders and spiderlings came to them for advice and help which is unusual in the spider world because they normally stick to themselves, if you know what I mean. Orb-weavers are found all over the world, in all countries of the world, but we are going to concentrate on a hedge in a back garden in Lowcliffe, near Christ Town in Dorset, England. This was the spider community that started the World Wide Web.

Garden spiders and spiderlings live anywhere there is grass and like to spin their webs or, as they call them, homes. If they can, they situate them in sun-drenched grassy areas with as little wind as possible. The problem with Lizzie's garden was that she lived at the top of a hill, not ten minutes' walk from the beach, and the wind would regularly whip up the hill from the sea, causing no end of issues for our young but intrepid spiders.

Now, I know that many boys and girls are frightened of spiders, but garden spiders are totally harmless. In fact, they do an awful lot of good in the garden because they remove the bugs, and it is the bugs that do the real damage. The way they keep the bugs down is by noshing down on them. It is a simple rule of life; spiders eat bugs and flies. There, I've said it. No going back now. So, we will just have to get used to Sid and Jayne having a supper of bug souffle.

The females can get quite big and grow to be bigger than the males, so while Sid was the big brother in age, he was the little brother in size. Nevertheless, he held seniority over his sister because he was the eldest, and as she was the only other one to survive the size-five boot of Big Eddie, Sid felt especially pressured to look after his little – not little, big, you know what I mean – sister.

The brother and sister spent most of their days spinning webs and then sitting in the middle of them waiting for lunch to come to them. Like when we order a Chinese takeaway, except we do not squirt venom into the driver and drag him into the house! As I said earlier, spiders are normally solitary creatures, but Sid and Jayne were different to normal and quite often went on adventures together.

On this day, they needed water because spiders need drink just like we do!

"Come on, Sid. Let's go to the birdbath in the middle of the garden," said Jayne. Knowing that Sid was more cautious than she was, she was off before she heard his answer, shouting back over one of her shoulders, "It's a lovely sunny day – let's go."

Sid scuttled along after her, sidestepping in and out of the blades of grass, trying to keep up with his larger sister, especially with her being luckier in the leg department, having one more than Sid.

He shouted, "Don't be so reckless, J. There are birds and cats and dogs and elephants and everything." He had to admit he was yet to see an elephant, but you never knew what you might see in the wilds of Lowcliffe. Jayne was away. Ducking, diving, scuttling, shooting a silk out and trapeze walking along it. The yards whizzed by until she was at the birdbath. She waited in the shade at the side of the acer tree, out of view of any predators. Panting but still going strong, Sid arrived thirty seconds later. His running motion was slightly lopsided, being a leg short, but over the months he had learned to cope. After all, if he did not cope, who would look after Jayne?

'Come on, slow croach' were the only words of encouragement he got. "Let's shoot a silk up there." The birdbath was an ornamental stone one with a single stone plinth that opened out into a stone bowl at about three feet high. Ornamental stone sparrows pretended to drink from the clear water put there that morning by Lizzie's mum.

Jayne used the expression, 'let's shoot a silk'. Now, that is spider talk, but what spiders normally have are four or more openings in their abdomen called 'spinnerets' from which they produce an exceptionally fine line of silk. As these are shot into space, they combine together to form one thicker line of web that immediately hardens as it hits the air.

Jayne shot a silk and started to climb up the thread when she heard her brother shout something from below. She was most of the way up, but exposed, when the light turned to shadow, and she realised from the flapping noise exactly what her brother had shouted.

Sid shouted again with all his might, "Jayne. *Crow!*"

CHAPTER 3

A GUST OF WIND

Jayne was so intent on getting to the top of her thread and slurping some fresh water on the hot summer's day that at first, she did not hear the shout from Sid. Her first real understanding that all was not well was when the sky started to go dark. And then darker, and then black. It was at this point that she heard her brother's pleas for her to beware. Looking above, she realised.

"*Crow!*" she shouted.

"I know it's a crow. I've been shouting, 'crow' for five minutes," said Sid.

The black devil swooped down to the water bowl and Jayne thought for a moment that it was just water the flapping creature wanted, but she was wrong. The bird landed on the lip of the basin, but instead of dipping its beak into the water, it swivelled round and aimed for the garden spider instead. Its large beak pecked hard in the general direction of Jayne.

She swung beneath her silk and shot another one onto the far side of the birdbath. Releasing from her first thread, she swung on the new one, whistling away but so close to the beak that she heard it snap in her wake. Meanwhile, down below, Sid was in a right old panic as his one and only sister swung beneath the basin and out of reach of the crow, at least for the moment. He started to shoot silks of his own like a Hollywood star in a World War II movie, firing off bullets.

Ping, ping, ping, the fine threads whizzed at the crow, one hitting him in the eye. The crow turned its head down to where the bullets were coming from and squinted at Sid with one eye closed, making him look like a pirate looking out to sea. The crow said in its squawking but chesty voice, "I can come back for her, but I'll eat you first, especially because you're so little." The crow flapped down to Sid, who started to edge around the other side of the tree, trying to keep the trunk between himself and the black death with a beak pecking at him. Now it was Jayne's turn to help her older brother. She had pulled herself onto the edge of the bowl and from her vantage point could see that Sid was not going to last much longer as he dashed back and forth on the other side of the acer. The crow was getting very annoyed, as picking off a couple of spiders should have been a lot easier than this was proving to be.

"Come here, you eight-legged freak," he said.

"Seven," Sid shouted back accurately, sounding like Len from *Strictly*. The crow jumped, flapped, skipped and had Sid trapped with his back to the bark. Gulping, he thought, *this is it*.

Jayne saw all this unfold three feet below her, and with no other option left open to her, she had shot a silk onto the crow's back and had scuttled down it. She was making her way down to the crow's head but was too small for the crow to feel her weight, and of course the crow was terribly busy catching Sid. The crow readied himself for the kill and Sid curled up in a ball with all seven legs wrapped around his abdomen.

The crow's head pulled back a fraction and then shot forwards, its beak opening slightly to peck and then open and eat Sid up or down. That was when Jayne made her move. She jumped off the top of the crow's head towards Sid, turning herself in the air, and shot two separate silks back at the crow's eyes. But she was not aiming for the eyes; she was aiming for the eyelids and, pulling with all her might, she swung downwards, pulling the eyelids down and giving the crow the biggest shock of his life so far. She also shouted 'Lolth' at the top of her voice which, as we all know, is the name of the Queen of the Spiders.

Now, just for a second, let us try and imagine what the crow felt like. Think of something hiding in your hair but much smaller than you, like a small mouse. It then jumps off your head, while at the same time shooting something at your eyes that sticks to your eyelids and pulls your eyes shut. Now I do not know about you, but I think I would be pretty upset if that happened to me. Actually, just the thought of a mouse hiding in my hair has made me need the toilet!

Anyway, back to Jayne who had landed on the top end of the crow's beak. Sid was still rolled up like a spider who was all rolled up. The crow was so shocked, he took to the air, rising quickly, dislodging Jayne. Her spider senses kicked into action, and she shot a thread at the underside of the beak as the crow took to the sky.

She screamed, but the crow was still too busy shaking his head to dislodge his eyelids to worry about a spider scream. Her thread started to get longer and longer as she released more and more from her spinnerets. She was dangling fifteen feet off the ground, but the crow was a further five feet above her and flying towards Lizzie's house. The crow was going to rise quickly to easily fly over the roof, but Jayne would be driven into the brick wall and be killed instantly. What could she do?

Her choices were hanging on and being splattered against the house wall or releasing herself from the thread and being splattered on the patio. She had no choice; she had to release, and so she did.

"No!" shouted Sid, recently unfurled. But his shouts were in vain; it was too late. Jayne was plummeting to her death.

And then, along came a gust of wind!

CHAPTER 4

HELP!

The wind caught the falling Jayne and swept her back upwards slightly and through an open window at the back of Lizzie's house. The crow vanished over the roof and Jayne swung straight into an upstairs bedroom while all Sid could do was hide behind the tree with his mandibles open like a barn door.

Now to be absolutely clear here, because I do not want all the spiders in the world to come knocking on my door complaining, spiders do not actually have mandibles; they have 'chelicerae'. The only animal to have these are spiders. Their chelicerae are like a pair of fangs. All other arachnids (that is a posh word for spiders) have a pair of pincers or scissor-like chelicerae. You know what they are like – hook-shaped fangs that jut out of a spider's face. In fact, they are the spider's jaws, and the only other type of animal with them are crabs or sea spiders. But they are not in the yarns of Sid Seven-Legs. Not *yet!*

But the point I am taking ages to make is that Jayne had been blown into the house and Sid saw it all and stood there with his mouth hanging open like a panting dog.

"Oh no. How do I rescue Jayne?" He said this out loud to no one in particular. He scuttled back to his rhododendron bush which was the home for hundreds of spiders and looked around for help from all his friends. It was at this point of his life that he worked out that the only friend he had was Jayne!

He went from web to web asking and begging other spiders to go with him to the house and help him find his sister, but no one would help him. Some spiders were mean to him because he had seven legs. One actually said, "Wobble there yourself, Stumpy."

And as I said earlier, spiders are solitary creatures that spend most of their lives sat in the middle of their webs waiting for dinner to arrive and perhaps stick around for a while. Spiders are always in lockdown because that is how they live. They rarely help each other. They do not band together in a time of crisis like the ants do. It's every spider for himself.

Also, the garden spiders rarely go indoors. Some do, those that live for many years, many being seven, as spiders do not live much longer than that. Even so, the general rule for garden spiders is they only go into houses if they have to.

This left Sid in a dilemma. He was still a young spider; he did not really know the world beyond the acer tree in the middle of the garden, and now he had to wander away on his own to try and find his sister in a world he had never been in before. A *house*.

Plus, he was one leg short of the accepted norm in the arachnid world. Even so, he did get one piece of advice from an old, fat spider that lived at the top of the bush. He was called Trevor. Sid was told by Trevor, "I've been in a house. Dangerous places them houses. Not like a garden. You're safe making a web in the middle of the bush, but don't make a web in the middle of the house. You'll be gone in a moment. Those humans don't like webs in the middle of their houses. Stick to the corners and get behind things if you can."

"Things? What things?" questioned Sid.

"Cupboards and beds and tellyvisuals and tables and chairs and other stuffs. But whatever you do, be careful of the bathrooms. They have giant waterspouts that can suck you under, three of them, sometimes four. Sunks, baths, shooers and something called a 'To Let'. That's the worst one as it stinks as well!"

Sid was grateful for any help he could get and so took this information on board from the kindlier than most Trevor. He turned away to continue his search for a spider to go with him when Trevor said one more thing.

"You won't get anyone to go with you, lad, who's been in the house before, as us garden spiders really don't like the indoors. Unless…" Trevor put a couple of hands on his head and scratched his abdomen with a third as he was deep in thought.

"Tell you what, lad. There's a spider who lives right by the main stem but in the soil on the ground. I've heard spiders say that she came from the house a couple of years ago. Something bad happened to her, but no one knows what. She lives even more on her own than the rest of us, but she knows the house. You never know your luck in a fly storm so you may as well try her."

Sid thanked Trevor once more and slid down a thread, disappearing amongst the leaves of the bush. Then Trevor's head appeared at the top of Sid's silk line and shouted down to him, "Do you not want to know her name?"

Sid, realising his stupidity, shouted back, "Of course, yes please, Trevor."

"You're going to like this, Sid. Her name is Mad Harriet."

"Mad Harriet!" echoed Sid. "Why in the name of Lolth is she known as Mad Harriet?"

Trevor just chuckled and said under his breath, "You'll find out, young Sid. You'll find out."

CHAPTER 5

MAD HARRIET

Mad Harriet was a 'Four Spot spider'. Four Spots are also orb-weavers but tend to live in long grass. Harriet was as old as spiders ever get; some said she had lived for over a decade, and she had bred many times over the years, with well over a thousand spiderlings, two hundred thousand grandspiderlings, over several million great-grandspiderlings, and I can't do the maths for the rest. No wonder she was mad – imagine having to remember to buy that many birthday presents. And Xmas must be a nightmare!

Sid was prepared to roll the dice and see if he could get a double six and persuade Harriet (known as Mad to her friends, but she didn't have any) to help him to enter the house and find his sister. You see, Mad Harriet, although she was a Four-Spotted Orb Weaver, had at some stage of her life lived in the house at the top of the garden. Sid thought she may be able to help him, but he did have to be careful because she had eaten several husbands over her lifetime. That sounds horrible, I know, but some spiders do that. I hope none do it in this story!

Sid knocked on Harriet's door. In the spider world, this meant he twanged the outermost thread of her web three times which transmitted to Mad H sat in the centre of it as *knock, knock, knock*. Mad H was about five times bigger than Sid, with a large, brown abdomen which from above looked like a farmer's cap. Towards the centre of the brown ring were four large, white spots that gave the spider their distinctive look and name.

Harriet raised her head and opened two of her eight eyes, glanced in the general direction of where the tweaks to her web had come from and shut them again. Orb-weavers tend to have four pairs of eyes in two rows of four. Two of them are used like we use ours to look at images; the other six are used to sense prey or predators by tracking movement or gauging distances. Despite having eight eyes, generally spiders do not have good eyesight and rely upon their sense of touch and feel as much as their eyes. Plus, they don't have eyelids, but we will come to that later!

Mad H either did not 'see' Sid or just decided to ignore him. Sid twanged again, *knock, knock* and then coughed in a way so that Harriet would have to acknowledge him.

"What?" she said.

"Well, my sister and only one and I've only got seven legs and the crow and the house and she's gone, and I need help and you and Trevor said you and and and…"

Sid ran out of words. It was an hour since Jayne had been blown into the house and that is like a day in spider time, so Sid was starting to panic and not making a lot of sense.

All Harriet said was, "And they call me mad!"

Sid calmed himself down and clearly said, "My only sister has been blown into the big house, and I'm going to rescue her. But I'm only just out of being a spiderling, and I've never been in the house before, so please can you help me?"

"Well, at least you're making sense now. Your sister, you say? In the house. Hmm, let me think. OK, I've thought. *No!*"

Sid wailed in despair.

"But I'm told you used to live there."

"I did," said Mad Harriet. "And it's dangerous in there. If you think crows are bad, humans are a hundred times worse. Your sister is gone, with Lolth in the underworld probably."

Sid continued pleading, refusing to believe that Jayne was dead.

"Please help me, Harriet; I'll do anything for you, absolutely anything, if you would just help me."

Harriet twisted her large, brown, bulbous abdomen round and strutted across her web with deceptive speed until she was staring into Sid's eyes, his eyes, his eyes, his eyes!

"Anything, anything at all."

Sid, realising he may have overcommitted, said, "Only if you will come with me into the house and show me the best way to find my sister. If we find her alive, I will be your slave for the rest of my life." Whatever spiders did with spider slaves is anyone's guess, but the promise certainly seemed to light a spark in Harriet's eyes, her eyes, her eyes, her eyes. (OK, I will not do that anymore.)

Harriet had heard something that interested her, but could she be trusted? Did Sid have any choice?

"You have a deal, an arrangement, a contract. We must exchange silk on it." The spiders both shot out a spiral of silk each that intertwined and Harriet then fastened to her web. This was the equivalent of them signing a contract, or a better comparison would be becoming *Blood Brothers*, a deal only breakable by death!

Only Arachne, the God of spiders, can break a silk oath that Sid and Mad Harriet had just made and the only way of seeing Arachne was... well, that is a story for another day.

Harriet had another plan. She had been meaning for the past couple of years to go back to the house. She had her own reasons for getting back. Many years ago, she had been wronged, and this was one of the main reasons why other spiders considered her as mad. She was full of anger and revenge, so much so that she often muttered and spoke to herself. There was something in the house that she had to deal with before she herself went to meet Arachne, and now she had the perfect sacrifice to take with her.

Sid knew none of this. He was only glad that Mad H had agreed to help. He did know that he had made an oath that was perhaps too big for him, but if it meant saving Jayne, he did not care. Saving his sister, if she needed saving, was the only thought in his head. What he did not know was that she was in tremendous danger. So much danger that if Sid had known, he probably would have given up!

CHAPTER 6

"COME ON, LET'S GO!"

Mad Harriet was packing, but spiders travel light. She scoffed, literally scoffed, down a couple of flies and one bluebottle she had been saving for a special occasion and then turned to Sid and said, "Come on, let's go."

Sid looked at the size of her and the ratio of her fat, brown abdomen and wondered how she would be able to walk. Mad H surprised him by being sprightly and nimble on thin legs that did not look as though they would hold her up, and he started to understand how she had lasted for so many years.

One thing Sid did know, though, was she was going the wrong way.

"Mad Harriet, where are you going?" he asked.

"Let's get something straight, Seven-Legs, you are not going to call me *mad*!" As she said this last word, she turned and showed Sid every one of her fangs in a snarl that made the hairs stand up on his legs and made him back away a few steps involuntarily.

"Yeah, yeah, OK. What should I call you then?"

"Just call me H," she replied.

"With a capital or just a little h?" Sid foolishly joked.

"With a *big* H," shouted H.

"Got it, got it. Big H. But back to my question, H," Sid stressed the H, so it was undoubtedly a big one, "why are you going the wrong way?"

"I'm not going the wrong way; I'm going a different way. Have you seen the lawn? It's a pigeon party down there. By the time they've finished with you, you'll be known as Sid No-Legs or perhaps just Ball. We are going off the top of the big shed, across to the acer tree, then onto the clothesline – shoot off the line to the barbeque and finally to the house. As I said what now seems like yesterday, come on, let's go."

"OK, H, I'm with you." Or so thought Sid, but Mad Harriet, or H, had been swinging around for a long time and Sid was still learning his trade as a webslinger, and he was about to get a lesson. H was as canny a spider as canny spiders get. Shooting several silks from her spinnerets at the same time, she was off and away. Up through the lower branches of the rhododendron, flying along single and double threads, she seemed to skip and jump up the tree like a kangaroo in the Australian desert.

Shooting a single thread out to the holly bush, she weaved her way amongst the prickles as though she was on a track and could not falter. From behind her, she heard Sid trying to keep up.

"Ouch, eeek, arggh, that's sharp, ow." As H got to the end of a large leaf furthermost from the centre of the holly bush, she launched herself into the air with almost reckless care for her own safety. She had to admit, she was beginning to enjoy herself. It had been a long time since she had been on a jaunt like this. She knew what she was doing as three silks shot from her body, forming into one long strand that flew downwards, attaching itself to a large padlock that was locking the shed.

Using the speed of her dismount from the holly leaf, she swung firstly downwards and then round in a large arc, and when it reached its peak, she detached herself from the silk and went shooting up into the summer sky, before landing with some aplomb on the roof of the shed. Sid was still stood on the leaf in the holly bush that Mad H had thrown herself off.

Once again, Sid started to understand why H was considered mad as she seemed to have no regard for her own safety. Sid took the longer route. He lowered himself down to the ground on a thread, scuttled across to the base of the shed and started the long climb up the wooden shed wall with a series of silks and his natural stickiness. It seemed to take forever, but after fifteen minutes or so, he got to where it had taken H fifteen seconds to arrive.

"This is going to be a very long adventure if you don't improve your silk skills," said H when he eventually landed on the shed roof.

"Don't you worry about me," said Sid, in a worried voice. "I might be slower than you at the moment, but I'll get better, and I'll keep going no matter what."

"We shall see. This next section is a lot more fun. I'm going to shoot a single silk down to the base of the tree. As we're up in the air, I'm going to allow gravity to do the rest."

"What's gravity?" asked Sid.

"If I were to push you off the roof and you didn't spin a web in time, what would happen to you?" H asked.

"I would fall all the way to the ground, and from the top of this shed, that would probably squish me."

"Well, that's gravity," said H. "Watch me."

H seemed to take a deep breath, if spiders can do that, and shot a long silk several feet across to the base of the acer tree. She then looped two of her 'hands' over the top of the thread and, turning to Sid, said, "See you on the other side." Before Sid could say, 'the other side of what?', H had looped her arms/legs over the silk and jumped off the shed roof. Sid was not aware, but it was a spider zip line, and H swept all the way down to the base of the tree. Oh, and she screamed all the way down.

"Your turn, Sid," she said from what looked like an awfully long way away in distance and, more importantly, in height. What Sid had yet to find out was that small spiders can drop from quite a height without doing much damage to themselves because they are so light. Some can even make a parachute-like web and sail the wind. Bigger spiders such as a tarantula can rupture their abdomens from a height of a metre and die in agony. There is no hard and fast rule, but the top of a shed was definitely over the limit that a spider of Sid's size should be taking a chance with.

Sid hooked two of his hands (three hands, four legs for Sid) and scrunched up seven of his eyes, peeping from the remaining one before launching himself into the air. Exhilarating was not the word for it. Breathtaking, spiderlicious, exciting, amazing, all these words still would not describe the thrill and rush of adrenalin that pumped through Sid's exoskeleton.

"*Yeeeeeesssssss*," he screamed on his way down. The air buffeted him around, but he held on grimly, loving every second. Just before he crashed into the tree, he disembarked, rolling himself into a ball, and rolled to the feet of H, who was simply stood there tapping one foot on the ground with two of her three arms crossed.

"Can I have another go please?" Sid had regressed into a spiderling again. Let us be honest, if spiders could be teenagers, that is the age Sid was at. So, he was not quite out of childhood yet, and if he had his own bedroom, you could guarantee it would be a mess.

"I thought you wanted to 'save' your sister," rebuked H.

"Yes, sorry, H. What's next?"

"We climb the tree and then do the same again from the tree to the clothesline so you will get 'another go' as you put it. Remember, this isn't a game, and if one of those pigeons see you, you'll be bird poo tomorrow!"

Lovely, thought Sid, deciding for once to keep his mandibles shut. Up the tree the two spiders went. Another zip line took them to the clothesline.

"Change of plan," said H. "Follow me into this pillowcase." Sid did as was asked of him.

"What are we doing in here?" asked Sid.

"We are about to be taken in with the washing. This will be a much quicker route into the house."

"But what if we get squashed in all the washing?"

"No chance of that – look, it's the male bringing the washing in. He doesn't fold it like the female. We will just get thrown into a basket and then, when inside, we will be able to make our escape." *She really does know lots about the house and the humans*, thought Sid. *She even knows the different behaviours of the males and females*. Sid had to admit, he was mightily impressed with H. If only he knew what she had in mind.

Lizzie's dad left the patio doors and walked over to the washing that had dried sooner than he thought in the strong June sunshine. *Great*, he thought, *get this in, get the beer out and the football starts in ten minutes. Perfect Sunday.* As H expected, he unpegged and, without too much thought, screwed the sheets up in a semblance of a fold but simply threw the T-shirts, pants, socks and, most importantly, the pillowcases on top of the rest of the washing. Squashing the pegs into his shorts' pockets, he picked the basket up, took it into the house and dropped it on the floor of the utility room. He left, closing the door behind himself using the ostrich philosophy that if he could not see it, it was not there.

"Made it," said H.

CHAPTER 7

BEHIND THE WALL

The utility room was dark with an overpowering smell of detergent and bleach. It is time for another spider fact. Spiders can smell even though they do not have a nose like mammals have noses. Spiders smell through the hairs on their legs. So, sadly for Sid, his sense of smell was not as good as other spiders who had managed to retain their full quantity of limbs. Spiders have specialised hairs along their legs that allow them to smell the objects they touch by interpreting the chemicals that make up the scent.

Even though Sid was a full leg of hairs short, the chemical smell was unusual to him, and he struggled to breathe in the air, especially as he was trapped under some bedding. Luckily, Mad H came to his rescue again.

"Come on, Seven, let's get out of here." She half-dragged, half-pushed Sid out of the pillowcase, through the strewn garments lying above them, until they got to the top of the pile. The smell was stronger out of the washing, but at least Sid could breathe in properly as there was more air on top than there had been underneath.

"Big breaths, Sid, come on, you can do this," H cajoled Sid until he stopped hyperventilating and got his breathing back to normal.

"That smell," he said, "what is it?"

"Humans use strong chemicals to get their stuff cleaned," said H. "Doesn't make much sense to us as we don't put things on our bodies like they put things on theirs. I have been told before that they don't like showing their real bodies off, but to be honest, Sid, I don't understand it myself. But that's what's making your legs twitch."

Changing the subject, she said to him, "Did you see where your sister went? Which window did she fly into?"

"It wasn't down here on the ground," said Sid. "She was high in the sky when the crow flew over the house, so it was one of the higher windows."

"Right," said H, "that means we have to get upstairs. It sounds to me like she went into where the humans rest. They call them bedrooms. It's like the centre of the web for us when it goes dark, and we rest."

This was all very educational for Sid. He would soon be an expert himself on houses and humans and stuff in them. *Bedrooms here we come*, he thought as H shot a silk and began to climb a cupboard in which sat a sink. A known black spot for spiders. Sinks were to spiders what quicksand was to humans. Once you were in, you rarely came out alive. Baths were worse as they were even more difficult to get out of, and the worst of all was a toilet. Throw a spider down a toilet and flush the chain is pretty much instant death.

H pulled herself up the silk pronto quick, and Sid followed, slower, but he was getting better at all this adventuring around. *Use it or lose it*, he thought, a saying that Jayne had often used when she wanted Sid to try something new.

"Where are we going now, H? I can't see a way out up there," exclaimed Sid, who was getting tired and could have done with a break to be honest. He had been on the go since first light, and it was now late afternoon, plus he had expended too much emotional energy for one day. H replied in her normal blunt, straightforward way.

"If you can't keep up, stop. If you can keep up, then do so, but shut up." *No empathy from Mad H*, thought Sid, who still thought of her as mad even if he did not say it. H carried on speaking.

"We are going behind the cupboards. Humans think that they fix these things tight to the wall, but they're rarely too tight for a determined spider to get behind. And I am a determined spider. Also, they drill into the walls, leaving tiny gaps between the fastenings and the cupboards that allow us to get behind the wall. Once we manage that, it's a straightforward climb to the rooms above with little danger from humans."

The two spiders took a couple of silks and swings to get themselves to the base of the next set of cupboards at human eye level on the wall over the sink. Being ultra-careful, they got to the top of the second level of cupboards in the utility room and made their way to the wall that they were fixed against.

Up at that height, over seven feet, and away

from the prying eyes of Lizzie's mum and dad, there was indeed a slight gap where the cupboard met the wall. To our eyes, there did not appear to be any gap at all, but the two spiders disappeared behind the cupboards and into the dark. Moments later, they found the screws that held the cupboards in place and, as predicted by H, they slid alongside the screw until they were behind the plaster and in the cavity wall of the house.

Now, even though H said there was little danger, I'm just going to provide you with a list of all the animals that have been found in the United Kingdom in the cavity walls of houses up and down the country. And all these are true.

Firstly, all kinds of birds have built nests in cavity walls by making their way in through the eaves. For example, robins, blue tits, sparrows, tree creepers, house martins, wrens, bluebirds, swallows and even a woodpecker once got into a house. These are just a few of the birds that can live in there.

There are also examples of the following insects: ants, cockroaches, ladybirds, woodlice, wasps and bees, all sorts of bugs – bedbugs, ladybugs, stink bugs and box elder bugs, flies and fleas and hundreds of spiders.

Now we get to the bigger animals; mice, rats,

foxes have been found in cavity walls along with cats and missing dogs and squirrels. In America, they can also get opossums and baby racoons finding their way into the walls.

Sid did not know any of this information, and H only knew about some of the dangers, but all these animals were a danger to spiders. Even house spiders did not like garden spiders that much. Therefore, when H said there was little danger at the back of the wall from humans, she was absolutely correct, but what she did not say was there was a whole host of other creatures that were very dangerous indeed!

Back to our intrepid duo. The spiders H and Sid commenced their climb up the inside of the wall. The house was a relatively new house, and the walls were pretty full of insulation material to keep the heat of the house inside and to stop the cold from getting in. It would have looked impassable to you and me but not to the spiders who, as they climbed, grabbed little bugs on their journey as way of a snack.

Sid was tired and not paying attention when he climbed directly into the back of H, who had stopped. She had stopped because she had arrived at her reason for coming back. She wanted to live back in the house again but had betrayed the king of the house in the past and needed an offering to make her comeback possible. The offering was to Rod, and Rod was the largest mouse you had ever seen. Not as big as a rat but not far off.

H intended offering Sid and his sister Jayne (if they found her) as peace offerings to Rod (Rod was short for rodent). Many moons ago, King Rod had used H as a lookout on a kitchen raid, but Harriet had left him to die and had escaped to save herself. She had always looked to get back to being a house spider but had never had the opportunity. Sid and Jayne were the opportunity she was looking for.

"Watch where you're going," said H. "When we find your sister, this is where we are bringing her back to."

"OK," said Sid, who really didn't have a clue as to the danger he was in.

CHAPTER 8

BATHROOM BREAK

We are almost at the point where we started this story. Do you remember? 'Sid's life was hanging by a thread'. Well, you now know most of how he got here. 157 brothers and sisters, but only one sister lived, thanks to Big Eddie; living happily with her in the rhododendron bush; wanting to be the big brother when unfortunately, because of spider gender sizes, he was the little brother; the crow; Jayne getting swished into the house; Trevor telling him about Mad Harriet; and finally the trip to the house via the washing line and basket and now the climb up the cavity wall trying to avoid dangerous predators such as King Rod! I hope you got all that because things are now going to get complicated!

H left the cavity wall and struck out across one of the wooden beams that were in the ceiling above the bathroom that was Lizzie's. Remember Lizzie? She is the little girl who lives in the house. Lizzie lived in quite a posh house in Dorset, and she had the family bathroom to herself because her mum and dad had one attached to their bedroom which H called an 'onsweet', probably because it smelled sugary.

H leapt off the beam and made her way to one of the light sockets that was embedded in the ceiling.

"Lots of room to squeeze through here for a fat spider," said H, and so she did. Squeeze through that is. Sid followed. They lowered themselves down from the bulb socket on long threads when in came Lizzie.

"Spider," she screamed, not realising there were actually two. H reacted much more quickly than Sid. She had been in situations like this before and knew the dangers of humans, even the little ones, so she was scuttling back up her thread to the bulb. Sid froze. Lizzie picked up the damp toilet brush and, while looking away because she was frightened of the little seven-legged spider, swung the wet brush in the general direction of Sid.

Sid's life hung by a thread! I told you we would catch up.

The toilet brush was spraying disinfectant everywhere as Lizzie waved it wildly above her head. Sid was lucky she was too scared to look where she was waving it. Nevertheless, Lizzie did manage to snap the silk that Sid was dangling off. He fell, hurtling towards the big basin that Trevor called a 'To Let' but we know as a toilet. Once Sid was in the toilet water, Lizzie would pull the handle, and no one had ever seen a spider again when that happened. They were gone – forever.

As he was falling, Sid remembered some of the web slinging he had done in the garden with H to get here and his muscle memory was good. Without thinking about it, his spinnerets shot out four strands of silk. The first flew aimlessly into the air. The second caught the edge of the bath but did not take hold. The third hit the rim of the toilet seat (yes, someone had left it up), and the fourth caught the porcelain of the toilet basin itself and that did not take either.

The only one that had stuck was on the top edge of the wooden seat that had been left 'up'. Lizzie was still swinging though and, opening her eyes and seeing the dropping spider (Sid), at long last actually aimed at him. Missing, she clattered the toilet seat which in turn slammed shut with an almighty bang, but this was when Sid's luck turned from bad to good.

As the toilet seat smashed down, it pulled the thread Sid had attached with it, which in turn pulled Sid away from dropping into the toilet and catapulted him across the room onto the bathroom floor. The floor was polished wood planks with tiny cracks between them, and without any more hassle, Sid plopped down into one of the cracks. The whole escapade had only taken ten seconds but felt like a day to Sid.

Lizzie's screams and banging had brought firstly her mum and then her dad rushing into the bathroom wondering 'what on earth was going on'. An expression that they both liked to use when Lizzie was just being a little girl.

"It was a massive spider," said Lizzie to her parents. "With fangs and everything, and it was dangling over the toilet, so I whacked it with the toilet brush."

"Well, that'll be the end of him then," said her dad. "And why is everything wet?" Deciding that if he stayed any longer, he would be asked to do something, he sort of faded out the door back to the telly.

"Come on, Lizzie, use our bathroom. It was probably just a little spider taking a toilet break," laughed Mummy. "He won't be coming back here again in a hurry. He must have some headache if you hit him with that brush. In future, shout me or Daddy, and we'll let the spider back outside. He can't hurt you, you know."

Lizzie stuck her bottom lip out in a pout and just said, "Hate spiders."

Sid was alive but trapped in a crack in a wooden bathroom floor and on his own. H had vanished back up into the gaps above the ceiling and Jayne was still nowhere to be found. Sid felt very alone, very frightened and at a loss as to what to do next. If spiders cried, then Sid cried just a little, but the situation was just about to change, for the better or the worse? I will let you decide.

CHAPTER 9

BAGGY

Baggy was a Ragamuffin, and a Ragamuffin is a type of cat that is predominantly black. Baggy was a beautiful cat with large, expressive eyes and soft fur, more like a rabbit than a cat. Baggy was Lizzie's cat. She had had her from a kitten and loved her dearly although, as she was getting older, she did not fuss over her as much as she once had done when she was just a youngster. I mean, she was seven now!

Ragamuffins are known for being good listeners and responding with soft purrs from deep in their throats. Ideal for children, they are placid in nature and respond well to love and affection, making them ideal companions. Baggy was short for Bagheera, the black panther from Kipling's *The Jungle Book*; Lizzie picked the name from her favourite Disney cartoon, even though Baggy was a boy's name in the cartoon. She did not much care for the live action one with the giant orangutan, and she thought they ruined the songs!

Baggy strutted into the bathroom, clearly the queen of this particular jungle. She came and went as she pleased, and even though she was a loving housecat to the family – especially Lizzie – she was also a good hunter and a keen mouser, should any venture in from outside, which they did from time to time. She spoke slowly and with a slight lisp, whistling on certain words. She addressed no one in particular but herself when she said, "Sooo, what is all the shouting and thcreaming about in here, I wonder?" She patrolled the outer edges of the bathroom, working her way around the back of the toilet and under the sink, occasionally stopping to sniff. She effortlessly sprung from the floor to the edge of the bath and then onto the sink in a second. Miaowing as she did so.

"No mices in here, no, no, no. No little animals at all. And yet I heard Litthie thcream. Why did she thcream?" And then she shouted, which came out as a loud, deep purr, "*Spider!* Yessss, spider is what I heard. So where is the eensy weensy spider?" She sprung back down onto the wooden floor, and even though she was agile, she landed with a thump. A thump that was directly next to where Sid was hiding, trembling between the boards. As Baggy landed with a thump on the board, Sid was catapulted from his hiding space and landed in a crumpled, seven-legged heap on the bathroom floor. Quick as a cheetah chasing a deer – after all, it is the same principle – Baggy pounced and landed a paw either side of Sid's body.

Nowhere to run from here, thought Sid, so, unfurling and looking up into the massive mirrors that were the cat's eyes, he said, "Alright, I'm Sid. I'm a garden spider, but I only have seven legs. Have you seen my sister?"

Baggy replied, "Alright, I'm Bagheera, but my friends call me Baggy. You can call me Bagheera. What doeth she look like, your thister?" (You already know that Baggy has a slight lisp and talks really slowly, so I'm going to write normally, and you can do the lisp in your head when you're reading it. That's how books work apparently.)

"Well," Sid said, "she's like me but bigger and has one more leg. Plus, she's great fun and frightened of nothing and always getting into scrapes. And I love her very much and miss her. Have you seen her?"

"Hmmm, let me see. Spider, like you but bigger, eight legs, you're not giving me much to go on here. Basically, you've just described every spider that's ever been in the house. And by the way, don't worry about her because I'm going to eat you anyway!"

"Eat me. But I'm tiny. I'm not big enough to get stuck in your teeth. There's more meat on a tulip than me and there's no meat on a tulip. I only want to find Jayne; that's my sister's name. Can you not give a tiny seven-legged spider a break?"

"You do have a point," purred the silky black cat. "But what can you offer me instead if I let you live?"

Sid instantly searched his pockets to see what he had before realising he was a spider and had no clothes on so had no pockets either. He said, "I can give you the opportunity to take part in a thrilling adventure helping me find my sister. As you just said, all spiders look the same so what chance do I have of finding her? We could go down in spider and cat history as the only ones to ever find a spider that's come in from the garden."

Baggy thought about this.

"I know this is a big deal for you with seven legs and whatnot, but looking for a spider isn't exactly going to get me on the front page of the *Daily Claw*.

I realise for a spider you'll probably be on the World Wide Web but not such a big deal for felines. How did you get this far anyway?"

Sid told his story from bush to bathroom, leaving nothing out, including Trevor, the crow and Mad Harriet.

"I see. There's another spider in here then somewhere?"

"Not sure where H went; she was up that thread like a rat up a drainpipe when the toilet brush started swinging."

"I have to admit, I'm intrigued," said Baggy. "Jump on. Let's do a tour of the bedrooms and we shall see if you can find… Jayne, did you say?"

"Yeah, Jayne. Fantastic. Thank you. Very very much. You're too kind. That's wonderful of you. It's not true what they say about cats. Cheers. Great. Amazing. Did I say thank you?"

"Get behind my right ear before I change my mind."

Sid clambered on board, which caused Baggy to wriggle about.

"Stop tickling," she said as she strutted out as regally as she had strutted into the bathroom.

What neither of them saw was H watching them carefully from behind the bulb in the ceiling.

CHAPTER 10

JAYNE

Jayne was frightened, hungry, tired, and lost. Apart from that, everything was fine. If you remember, we left Jayne just as she was flying through the air, and do not forget, spiders are not really built to fly through the air and into the house via an open window. She landed quite comfortably on a bed. She was in the main bedroom and had landed on the double bed of Lizzie's mum and dad.

Her spidery instincts kicked in, and she knew she could not sit out there in the open. A human would soon be throwing all sorts of things at her if she stayed where she was, and so she scuttled her way to the edge. I say scuttled, but getting across the bed for a spider was like walking on a bouncy castle for Lizzie, and so she bounded across the bed rather than scuttled. In other, less threatening, circumstances, she may well have had some fun bouncing around, but now was not the time for fun.

Dropping a silk over the side, she dropped from the bed to the bedroom floor. Without thinking, just reacting, she saw the dark shadows under the bed and moved from the light to the dim interior of the world beneath the bed. She immediately felt a lot more comfortable and less exposed. She moved towards one of the bed legs closest to the wall, quickly spun a web for herself and climbed into the comfort of its centre to give herself some thinking time. That is the great thing about spiders – they carry their home with them wherever they go and can set a new one up in minutes.

OK, what's next? thought the erstwhile, intrepid spider. *I'm frightened, hungry, tired and lost, but apart from that, fine.*

I wonder what Sid is thinking. Where is he? Will he try and help me? Will he get home OK? Even in her most testing of times, Jayne's thoughts firstly turned to her brother. Even as she was thinking this, Sid was on his way back to the rhododendron to try and get help. He was hours away from meeting Baggy yet. When spiders do not eat, they get tired and lethargic, and with the trauma that Jayne had faced with the crow and flight into the house, her eight eyes soon closed, and she fell into a deep, restorative sleep.

Now when I say she closed her eyes, she actually did not close her eyes because, and do not let this gross you out, spiders do not have eyelids. Their eyes therefore do not close when they sleep because they do not sleep like us either. Their bodies slowly start to reduce activities and their metabolic rate slows down. They go into a sort of trance, but their eight eyes stay open. Whichever way you come at it, Jayne was taking a well-earned nap.

She stayed that way for several hours before her abdomen began to move more rapidly, and her body awoke from its rest. While she was sleeping, several woodlice had been trapped in her recently spun web and so late lunch had arrived. A crunchy but nutritious meal.

That's better, she thought, *now to make a plan.* Jayne always believed having a plan was a good idea. It focused the mind during the day when times got tough, and they certainly did not get any tougher than they were right now. That is not absolutely true, as they were about to get tougher.

"Hey."

Jayne spun around but could not see where the voice had come from.

"Psst. Hey, sister."

Where was that coming from and who thought they could call her sister apart from Sid?

"Over here. Bottom of the skirting board."

Jayne looked into the shade behind the front of the bed and noticed what looked like scuff marks across the boards, but at closer inspection, she could see that the board had been cut away slightly at the bottom. Not so that you could see much if you were a human, but a gap had been created between the skirting board and the floorboard. From the deeper shadow, two fat pink eyes peeped out. So dark they were almost red, like dried blood.

"Here. See me? Come to me."

Jayne sprung from her web and landed several feet away from the eyes, thinking to herself, *why would I go to them?* Instead, she stood her ground and looked around, planning her escape should one be required. She said bravely, "Show yourself, creature. Let me see who I'm talking with."

"Sister, get here now. If I have to come for you, you will regret it."

Jayne held her nerve, but she would have been lying if she had said her nerves weren't getting a little frayed around the edges. She spoke again. "I don't expect you to come for me." As she said this, she thought to herself, *for me? What does that mean?* She continued, "But if you just show yourself then we can talk properly, and I will come to you when I know who I'm dealing with."

"Dealing with. You are dealing with a *king*." The blood pink eyes flamed when the creature in the skirting board shouted this last word.

A king? King of what? thought Jayne. She almost asked that very question but thought better of it. Instead, she would play along.

"Your majesty, please forgive me. I did not know I was speaking with royalty. You have my humble apologies. I am but a mere garden spider who has been whisked into your majesty's house and is lost and frightened. Because I am frightened, I am unable to approach. If you were just able to show yourself then we could talk."

Jayne wondered if she had been too accommodating and had sounded sarcastic but then the eyes moved forwards. Firstly, a bulbous black nose pushed through the gap. Followed by a badly scarred snout with broken whiskers. Then the pink eyes and two broad, meaty shoulders and finally a thick, grey, matted, furry body with a large, white stomach but big muscular back legs.

It was without doubt the biggest mouse Jayne had ever seen.

"Your majesty," she stuttered and actually tried a little bow, which just looked odd on a spider. The oversized mouse stared her down and said, "I'm King Rod, and you're trespassing in my kingdom."

CHAPTER 11

KING ROD

Now I have to tell you one or two things about King Rod. His name was only really mouse number twenty-three as his mother never bothered with names. She never bothered with names because she had so many offspring so frequently and could not keep track of them all. Rod found out from an early age that he was a 'rodent' and so dropped the 'ent' and became Rod. He added the 'King' part of his name once he took control of the 'Edge World'. The 'Edge World' is everything in a house a human cannot see.

There is not a lot of difference between a 'house mouse' and a 'garden or wood mouse', but Rod had started as a garden mouse who had heard about 'The Edge' and wanted to be part of it. Even so, garden mice are slightly bigger than house mice and have a browner cast to their fur. Rod was the biggest of all, so big he was sometimes thought of as a small rat rather than a large mouse. This had certainly helped him in his journey from outside to be King of the Edge.

Let me give you some facts about Rod and field mice in general. They have large eyes and ears and a long snout. Mostly brown, they can be grey or a mixture of the two, but normally they all have white bellies. They are cautious mice, until they get as big and confident as Rod, and are always sniffing about. Field mice are great leapers and so have extraordinarily strong, large back feet. They eat berries, seeds, insects, and some humans say mice will eat anything. Most house mice smell strong, an earthy, pungent smell, but field mice carry virtually no odour. So, one thing you could say about Rod was he was not smelly!

A fact that most people do not know is that mice are aggressive creatures and often there are fights amongst themselves. When he lived outside in the garden, Rod was a top draw at the weekly mice fights held under the shed. The mouse who organised all the bouts was called Reedy, and he challenged mice from wide and far to take Rod on under the shed on a Saturday night.

Mice came from as far as Harbinger Road, which was three streets away, to challenge Rod, 'The Mouse King of the Ring', to try and take his title. Rod, who had been the largest in his family, had had to fight for every morsel of food as he was growing up; after all, he was one of twenty-four. His mum had given birth to four litters of six pups each before she had gone to the great cheese in the sky. It was a competitive upbringing that Rod was born into, but what he lacked in brains, he more than compensated for in size. He was born big and that gave him the chance to get bigger, and he took that chance with all four paws.

Back to Saturday nights and Reedy's fight fests. Field mice do not normally get through the winter months if they stay outdoors, as the weather gets too cold for them and they go off to the big cheese in the sky, but if they can get indoors, they can live for four or even five years. Two years ago, in Rod's first summer, was when he became the 'Mouse of the House; the Head of the Shed; the Southpaw Paw and the 'Mouse who could splat a Rat'. These were all names that Reedy gave him to get the crowds in. Entrance fees were either an acorn, three berries or a piece of bread, and Rod got his prize paid to him in food. But to be honest, Rod was in it for the glory, the glory and the fact that he really did enjoy a good scrap.

We will now go to the night of his last fight, long before Sid or even Sid's mum had even been born. It was one of those overcast June evenings when the sky started to darken early as the squally rainclouds, blackened and heavy with prospective rain, came in off the sea and made their way inland. Hot and 'hummid', as Lizzie would say, there was electricity in the heavy air.

Reedy stood in the centre of the ring. The day had been hot before turning for the worse, and there was a good mischief of mice (that's what you call a group of mice, cool name), at least thirty, and one or two squirrels in the crowd. It was going to be a testing night tonight for Rod as he was up against Mighty Mike from Laburnum Crescent. Mighty Mike had a similar reputation to that of Rod but in his own street. Rod was big; Mike made him look small.

Rod's supporters were looking anxious, their eyes sticking out on stalks, which they did anyway! Someone in the crowd shouted, "Check his paperwork. He's as big as a rat." The crowd was getting restless but the squirrels, who spent all day bouncing around the oak trees, were acting as bouncers and quietened down the unruly ones. The mice taking bets were having a 'field day' as, for once, Rod's favourite tag might prove fruitful for them. Reedy made his way over to Rod's corner.

Rod whispered to Reedy, who doubled as his trainer, "He's big. What do you think?"

Reedy replied, "Belly, Rod. Always go for the belly. Less fur. Not as thick, lots of pain. No one likes their belly bitten."

Rod nodded, which was hard to do as a mouse's head goes directly into his body, but Reedy knew he understood. Reedy went into the centre of the ring and announced the fight.

"Does, bucks and any pups who have got in tonight. Fighting in the oak corner, all the way from Laburnum Crescent, fighting out of the Farmer Giles stable, weighing in at as big as a rat, the challenger, put your paws together for Mighty Mike."

There were a few whoops from his corner but nothing more. Rod was fighting at home.

"Fighting in the fir corner, all the way from the other side of the shed, fighting out of Reedy's nest, the undisputed Mouse of the House, King of the Ring, Champion Mouse of the Known World in Lowcliffe, I give you King Rod."

For once, Rod looked nervous, especially as a huge roll of thunder rumbled overhead. Reedy shouted, "It looks like it's getting ready to *rumble.*"

CHAPTER 12

STORM'S COMING!

Rod was not used to being the smaller mouse in these fights and normally overpowered his opponents with brute strength, pinning them to the ground until they submitted or knocking them senseless with a cuff around the head. Tonight, he was going to have to be a little cleverer than normal, a state of mind that did not come naturally to him. So instead of running into battle as fast as he could, he was cautious, stood back and let Mighty Mike come to him.

Under the shed, the squeaks from the mischief of mice who were the paying audience were loud and bounced and echoed off the wooden boards that was the floor of the shed. The thunder continued to rumble above them and was so loud, the small building seemed to shake. Every now and then, all the mice snouts lit up and froze, as though posing for a photograph, as a line of lightning raced across the dark sky and its remnants found its way to the shadows below. All in all, it was an overly dramatic scene. Meanwhile, Mike was swinging thumping blows at Rod but not in a constructive manner, enabling Rod to dance out of the way and for the moment remain unharmed.

"Get on with it," someone squeaked from the crowd. "Me and me brother fight harder than this."

Even Reedy shouted to the two combatants, "Come on, lads, give 'em a fight. I won't be able to sell the next one if you don't get to it."

Rod moved in. Standing proud on his back two feet, he cuffed Mike once, twice and a third time with quick sharp blows to the head, but the smacks did not seem to have much effect on Mike. Mike roared back. He stayed on all fours and ran hard at Rod, hitting him square in the smaller mouse's tummy and knocking him backwards in a mouse version of a rugby tackle. Being on your back was not a position you wanted to be in during a mouse fight as your soft underbelly was exposed. Rod flipped quickly onto all fours, but Mike was still on Rod, biting down on his exposed back of the neck.

The bites were superficial as mice have thick fur over the top of their backs to better protect them from predators, but Mike did taste blood and, gripping Rod hard, flung him like a dog with a bone across the ring. Rod rolled and, using his greater agility, gained his back feet again and sprung into the air, coming down hard, feet first, onto Mike's back, knocking the wind out of the bigger mouse. Rod was getting the upper paw and, seeing his opponent gasping for breath, burrowed his snout beneath Mike and flipped him over onto his back. He saw his chance to bite and dove onto the exposed white belly.

But Mike was big, and as Rod tried to nip and bite, Mike hit him hard several times across the snout, drawing blood and making deep gouges in it, gouges that years later, Jayne would see as scars criss-crossing King Rod's face in the bedroom of the house. That, though, would be years later, and Mike and Rod were now in a ferocious battle for survival. The crowd were cheering and shouting for their favourite; thunder boomed, shaking the shed on its foundations, and the rain started to come down. Not a trickle first, or a build-up starting with a shower, the rain went from none to downpour instantly, battering onto the wooden structure and stopping everyone in their tracks. The crowd silenced and the two fighters, for a moment, paused in their bloody battle.

All round the shed, the ground shook with the weight of the rain, and the previously dry soil burst upwards and outwards as though hundreds of tiny explosions were taking place. It was then that the black cat, who we know as Bagheera or Baggy, erupted under the shed and the world of mice turned red.

"*Cat*," screamed several mouse voices at once as Baggy turned this way and that, overwhelmed with the choice of so many prey to try and catch. She spun round in circles under the shed as the mice ran in all directions. It was more a game for Baggy but was a matter of life or death for the brown and grey field mice. Rod decided not to hang around; he and Mike could renew pleasantries at a later date. His priority now was to make sure he got to that date.

He ran out into the sheeting rain, which hit him so hard it knocked him off his feet. Skittering across the lawn, he headed for the only thing he could see in the rain which were the lights of the house. Racing across the garden, he heard the screams and chaos behind him as Baggy did what all cats do with mice all over the world, but for this story, we do not need the details. He ran as though the devil had his tail and approached the lights with less fear than he held for what was behind him.

How could he get in? He knew little about the ways of a house. To him, under the stormy sky, it looked like an impenetrable barrier made of bricks, a substance he knew he would not be able to gnaw through. Lightning struck, and he quivered with the bright expanse of light that lit everything up. Looking behind him as the fork jagged the heavens in two, he saw his biggest fear. Running across the lawn towards him was Baggy, not running, hunting!

He turned back to the house; there had to be a way in. A voice from the Gods saved his life; it was a little house mouse peeping from between two bricks above the drainpipe.

"Quick, mate, jump in here." And so, Rod did.

Baggy slid into the back of the house, bumping her black nose as Rod entered the world of 'The Edge' for the very first time.

CHAPTER 13

JAYNE AGAIN

Let me remind you where we left Jayne. She was under the bed of the main bedroom in the house and had just met King Rod for the first time. We now know that it was over two years since Rod had first entered the house as a field mouse but had managed, through his size and fighting prowess, to turn himself into the King of The Edge. The Edge is everything in a house that we humans don't see on a day-to-day basis. So, the lowly field or garden mouse had become the ruler of the house, including any house mice that dared to live under his rule.

Mad Harriet, remember her, had also got some form of a 'deal' going with Rod before leaving the house under a shadow, having left Rod to fend for himself in a do-or-die situation. And our hero Sid, well where's he in all of this? Don't worry – all will soon be explained as that's my job, and you don't have to worry. But Jayne was worried as the blood pink eyes had come from behind the skirting board and were eyeing her up in an unpleasant manner.

Jayne was mesmerised by the sheer size of the mouse. Mice are much bigger than garden spiders anyway, but this King Rod was the size of a lorry in relation to a human child. He repeated his statement.

"I am King Rod, and I repeat – you are trespassing. Do you have anything to say for yourself?"

"No not really, your majesty. My name is Jayne and I don't intend staying here long if I can help it, and it's not my fault I'm here. A crow and the wind had a greater say in my circumstances than I did."

Behind Rod, another mouse had come out of the gnawed hole and whispered something in Rod's ear that Jayne could not hear. She heard one or two words but couldn't make sense of them: 'spider', 'webs', 'trap', 'food'. What did mice want with spiders? They might occasionally eat one if they get too close, but the unwritten rule was that spiders and mice left each other to their own devices and rarely got involved. Even so, Jayne was feeling uneasy.

Rod spoke again.

"This is one of my subjects, Whispering Wilf. We call him that because he whispers and is called Wilf."

"Makes sense," said Jayne.

Rod ignored Jayne and continued.

"He is one of my better thinkers. He thinks and I bully. It's a good split of skills because if he thinks something he shouldn't, I can always bully him as well. He, he, he."

Jayne saw that Rod was trying to be funny so giggled like a spider. Have you ever seen a spider giggle? No, neither have I, but Jayne definitely giggled, or at least pretended to.

"Wilf has reminded me that we need good spiders. We never have enough spiders, and a large female such as yourself will be good for our stock."

"Stock? What do you mean stock?"

"Did I say stock, sorry I meant to say team. Yes, team, that's a better word. We need you on our team, Jayne. Wilf here has had some good thoughts over the years and the spider team was one of them." This wasn't absolutely true, but Rod had no problem lying to get what he wanted.

"I'm sorry, your majesty, but I have no idea what you're talking about. I have to go now, but it was good meeting you."

Whispering Wilf was a tiny mouse. Half the size of Rod. He was also a house mouse. Very grey with a tail as long as his body and protruding wide eyes that seemed to be his entire face. He was thin, he liked to think he was wiry, but he was definitely thin. Thin and quick. Too quick for Jayne, especially as she had turned her body and was walking away.

Wilf moved as fast as lard in a frying pan and as silently. He was away from Rod's side, had snatched Jayne up in one of his strong paws (using his sharp claws to keep a tight hold) and was back at Rod's side as quick as you could say, 'hey, what are you doing?'.

Rod spoke. "OK, take her to the others. She's a good size, this one, and ready for having spiderlings. The stock, or should I say team, will soon be back up to the right numbers. There is only one animal who can challenge me in this house, and with the help of the spider stock, she can be defeated as well, once and for all, and when she's dead, there's no one to stop me."

Jayne was caught tight and didn't struggle for fear of getting damaged. A spider in a mouse's claw is not a good place for a spider to be as spiders' legs can be quite fragile. Just ask her brother Sid. Rod squashed back through the hole and Whispering Wilf followed.

It was about thirty minutes later when Baggy the Ragamuffin black cat slunk into the room with Sid Seven-Legs sat behind one of her ears. What Baggy didn't know was King Rod was trying to kill her and was using hundreds of spiders to help him. Rod had made a spider prison in the underworld of The Edge and was using the spiders against their will to catch, not a fly like the nursery rhyme but a cat! And Baggy was that cat, who was soon to become an endangered species. Rod and Baggy had history, and the king was going to end it!

CHAPTER 14

BAGGY AND SID

"Baggy, can you take me over to the window please? I want to see the view from here."

"Do you have time to be looking at views?" asked the laconic cat.

"I'm not looking at the view, but by looking through the window I'll be able to see if this is the one that Jayne got swept into," replied Sid.

The cat effortlessly sprung onto the windowsill and straight away Sid could tell by looking at the position of the tree in the centre of the garden that this was indeed the room that Jayne had been swept into.

"This is it. No doubt," said Sid. "She must have landed on the bed." Once again, Baggy obliged, landing sure-footedly in the middle of the mattress. She curled up contentedly.

"Hmm, this is nice. Hot sun, hot bed, nice and soft, late afternoon doze."

"I don't have time for that," Sid said as he leapt from the edge of the bed and slid down a thread quickly to the floor. "I have to find Jayne. Not go to sleep." Sid didn't know but he was only thirty minutes behind Jayne now as she had already had an afternoon sleep. He was only thirty minutes behind, but she had been dragged against her will into The Edge, so he had to do more than catch her up. He also had to free her from the clutches of King Rod, the sworn enemy of Baggy, who was at this point purring in a light sleep like the motor of a Harley Davidson.

Sid walked under the bed and let his eight eyes adjust to the change in light. He knew that had Jayne landed on the bed, she would have done exactly the same. Spidery instincts and all that! Plus, he knew his sister would want to get out of the light before a human walked in. Swinging hand over hand like Tarzan in the films, he trapezed his way around under the bed, using the wooden bed slats to stick his silks on. It wasn't long before he saw the web left behind by his sister. Sid knew it was Jayne because she had left her trademark. An elaborately embroidered letter J in the bottom left-hand corner. She had always done this since being a spiderling and finding some other spider had stolen her web and, more importantly, the prey she had caught. Ever since, she had signed off like Picasso with a painting. Without thinking about it, she had left Sid with a clear indication this is where she had been. Moments later, Sid found the entrance to The Edge that Jayne had been dragged into against her will.

Sid dashed back to his large, furry, black friend on the topside of the bed.

"Baggy, I've found her."

Dragging one eye open like a trapdoor to a cellar, Baggy sleepily lisped, "Found her. Where? And where is she then?"

"Sorry, OK. Found her, meaning I know where she is. Was. Her web is under the bed. She's not. Not now." Sid wasn't making much sense in his excitement.

"Hop back on," said Baggy. "Let's go and see." So, Sid did.

Sid directed Baggy to the front underside of the bed and pointed out the web and Jayne's monogrammed calling card letter J.

"See, look there, Baggy – Jayne always signs off her work."

"Who does she think she is, Banksy? She's only made a web."

"I know," said Sid, "and we can argue later about a web being a work of art or not, but the point is, she was here, and this web is fresh, so she was here not that long ago, and look over there. A gap that goes under the floorboards. It looks like it's been gnawed through by something."

"And I can guess what that something was," replied Baggy. "We have quite a few mice kicking around this house (Baggy said mithe but I said I wouldn't write like that anymore) and one in particular who claims to be the King, not only of the mice but of the whole house, or at least The Edge."

"What's The Edge?" asked Sid.

"It's everything the humans can't see or don't want. It's the cavity walls; it's under the floorboards; it's the loft, the inner brick structure – it's The Edge. It's behind that hole there. That so-called King Rod calls it his kingdom."

Sid looked at Baggy from within his eight beady eyes and said, "I have to go in there, Baggy. I have no choice. That must be where Jayne has gone. Us spiders like little nooks and crannies like in there."

Baggy answered, "But surely she wouldn't go in there if she was trying to get back to the garden?"

"I think she would. She doesn't know her way around this house. It's much easier for her to spin her way down there to the garden than it is for her to navigate herself around the human part of the house. I didn't know it was called The Edge, but I knew there wouldn't be any humans down there and that's safer than out here."

Baggy shook her head, and a wave went down her sinuous body as though she was being stroked by an unseen hand.

"I think you are wrong about it being safer, Sid. Spiders go missing in this house, never to be heard of again. You don't know King Rod, but there are all sorts of stories about him and his mischief of mice and what they do to other creatures. We all have to eat, and it's in all our natures to hunt or be hunted, but what Rod does is unnatural. Mice are not supposed to behave the way he does. Sometimes I think he thinks he's almost human."

Sid shook his body because it's hard for a spider to shake his head. You know how you feel when you see a big spider and a shudder runs through you, well, that's what Sid felt like when he heard that a mouse thought he was human.

It's the biggest sin an animal can make – being human.

"I still have to go, Baggy. If Jayne is in there, then she's my only sibling left alive, and I have to protect her or be prepared to die trying."

"As you say it, my brave little friend. If you find her, make your way down to the cellar and I will meet you there. I will check once a day. When we meet again, you can jump behind my ears, and I'll transport you both back to the garden." Baggy's sentiments were easily said, but the truth of what was to happen would be vastly different indeed.

They quickly said their farewells, and Sid entered The Edge.

CHAPTER 15

H AND THE EDGE

The only creature we have not checked in on for a while is the grand old lady of the spiders, Mad Harriet, or as she is known to her friends, H. We left H scooting back up a thread into a light socket as Lizzie tried to knock Sid's remaining seven legs off with a toilet brush. She's now peeping out of her eight eyes down at Sid as adult humans arrive and Sid hides in a crack in the floorboards. Eventually, she watches as Sid leaves with his new feline friend Baggy.

Harriet works her way back to the loft space, builds herself a web and contemplates what her next move is going to be. She knew about the spider slaves that King Rod keeps; after all, she used to be the chargehand of them. The best way to describe a chargehand under these circumstances is that she used to be the 'boss slave'. Rod left H to manage the spiders, and she had a series of large female spiders called 'Eighters' to keep the rank and file in order. In other words, she had betrayed her own spider race to her own personal benefit.

She was King Rod's right-hand spider and, apart from Whispering Wilf, was the most important part of The Edge hierarchy. That was until she had scarpered to save herself when Baggy had King Rod cornered. Unfortunately for her, Rod made a miraculous escape and, knowing she would never be forgiven, H went to live her life in the garden rather than The Edge. Sid showing up, especially after such a long time had passed, made her think that by making a peace offering of Sid and Jayne to the King, she might be able to get her old job back. After all, Jayne was a young, strong, large female whom Rod could farm to produce many other spiders for his army.

She contemplated her predicament and she calmed herself down and went into a spider sleep where her mind wandered. She knew she had lost

Sid to Baggy but also knew that Sid wouldn't leave the house until he found Jayne. So, she had to find Jayne first. Plus, she knew why Rod had his spider army and what he one day hoped to achieve with them. Rod was without recourse the King of The Edge but wasn't satisfied with just The Edge. Rod wanted to be king of the whole house. To do that, he had to get rid of Baggy, the one animal that Rod probably would lose out to in an animal scrap.

The spiders were, and had been for a long time, part of Rod's master plan to get rid of Baggy once and for all, and then he could become the King of the House. H wanted to be back in the fold in time to reap the benefits of being close to the King. She planned to do that by handing Sid over to Rod, along with Jayne. But Sid had gone. And where was Jayne? She needed something else to bargain for her life with Rod.

She was sat in her web – dozing, thinking, plotting – when she heard the unmistakable noise of a cat snoring. That deep sonorous purring that made the hairs on her legs stand to attention like ants in a line. Moving across the beams in the attic space, she saw Baggy jump off the bed and disappear beneath it. She didn't clock Sid sat behind the Ragamuffin cat's ear.

H, knowing that Sid couldn't be far away, gently lowered herself down on such a thin silk it was almost translucent. She landed gently on the bedstead and listened hard. She heard snippets of the conversation between Sid and Baggy and then watched as Baggy left the bedroom alone with the promise that she would meet up again with Sid in the cellar.

H waited five minutes before she too lowered herself to the underside of the bed. Moving around, it didn't take her long to find Jayne's old web and then the gnawed mouse hole giving her access to The Edge. She also had the information that would get her back into Rod's good books. She knew where Baggy was going to be to meet Sid, in the cellar, which is where Rod could set his trap. The trap that would be prepared by his spider army, which H would suggest she led again.

It would be a tricky negotiation as Rod rarely listened to anyone else apart from his own voice, but H was a tricksy old spider and could spin a yarn or two herself. She could do this, talk her way back into the royalty. Sid and Jayne, if she could ever catch up with them, would still be sweeteners to the deal, but Baggy was the big prize. Get rid of her and Rod would get his wish and rule the house. All these plans sped through Mad Harriet's little brain in the time it takes to shoot a thread. So, approximately fifteen minutes after Sid had stepped through with dread and trepidation, and fully forty-five minutes after Whispering Wilf had dragged Jayne in, H stepped into the world she once helped to rule.

H stepped back over and into The Edge.

She also had advantages that no other creature had at their disposal. She had lived there before and, being a spider as opposed to a mouse, she could get through gaps and holes and places where there were no gaps and holes. She knew the best way to get around. She was once in control of all the spiders in The Edge and had spies everywhere who had told her all the secrets of The Edge. She could move around like a ghost, appearing and vanishing like a phantom singing opera in a large theatre. Effectively, she was an invisible spider.

Rod would be glad to have her back. Or so she thought!

CHAPTER 16

SID SEVEN-LEGS

Right, let us get back to our hero, as I think we've been talking a lot about others in this story and, after all, it is called the Yarns of Sid Seven-Legs not the tails of King Rod. Sid crept into the mouse hole at the front of the bedroom and stole slowly along the gap behind. He didn't have too many choices. Up took him back to the loft; right or left would take him around the outside of the bedroom he had just left, but down would take him to a different floor of the house. He thought that Jayne would make her way down but could not see any evidence that she had gone that way. He thought he might see a thread that she had used to drop down but no thread.

Jayne had gone downwards but unfortunately grasped in the claws of Whispering Wilf. Sid noticed there were many mouse droppings littering the brickwork as he shot a thread and made his descent. *They really have a mouse problem in this house*, he thought as he dropped. Little did he know how much of a problem, a problem that very soon was going to become his as well.

The house Sid was in was a relatively new one. It had been built approximately five years ago and therefore the insulation was good, and the walls were stuffed with insulation material which is like a thick, course wool, making it difficult for animals to move around in, but Sid could see tunnels everywhere which he assumed correctly were made by the same mice that left their droppings everywhere. The house was big, with five big bedrooms and a study and a living room and a den and a family room and a kitchen and four bathrooms and a utility room and a patio and an attached garage, and and and, it was a *big* house! And it had a cellar! Unusual for new houses.

Sid didn't know any of this. He had an idea it was a big house just from looking at it from under his bush in the garden, but whenever he looked in that direction, it seemed like another world to him. As from today, it was now his world as well but a world which he did not know. He plopped down, landing on a broken piece of cement outside the downstairs bathroom. Not that he knew that; to him, he was in a maze of tunnels through cavity walls filled with scratchy, dense wool. Luckily for him, the tunnels had been well constructed and worn with use, making it possible for him to shoot, swing, shoot again, swing and make his way through them.

This he did to great effect but without knowing where he was going, and after thirty minutes, he was totally lost. Outside, the sun was setting as the summer's day was drawing to a close. He had spent all day on his adventures with little to eat and no rest. He was in a tunnel by the living room that was bigger than the others he'd been swinging down but was yet to meet anyone or anything. He had heard some squeaks, but the sound travelled through the tunnels in a strange way, and he found it difficult to trace the source of the squeaks. It was time to rest, and as the tunnel opened up into a chamber that could have held a small mouse meeting, he crawled into the top corner of the room, spun himself a web and promptly fell asleep. (Don't forget he has no eyelids so fell asleep but with his eyes wide open.)

Time passed, and as he slept, his body recharged, and as an added bonus, some small plaster bugs got caught up in his web. When he woke, he took the opportunity to refuel with the bugs as well as recharge with the sleep. He heard squeaks again.

"I have to talk to someone and see if Jayne is down here somewhere," he said to himself just as two little grey house mice went scampering through the chamber he was in. He was about to shout to them when he heard one of them say, "He's got a new spider. Going to breed her, he is."

To which his companion, a doe, replied, "Bloody spiders. I 'ate 'em. He 'as 'em everywhere. Thinks more of them spiders than he does of us."

Sid stopped himself from shouting and decided to follow the mice instead. They left the chamber, taking a sharp left, then a right and entered a long tunnel. Sid ran along the roof of the tunnel above their heads and behind them so they couldn't see him. This was when he realised that since he'd been in The Edge, he hadn't seen one spider or even evidence of a spider. There wasn't a cobweb in sight. He would have thought there would be lots of house spiders living in the walls but seemingly not.

Really strange, he thought as his seven legs clattered along like spokes of a bicycle as he struggled to keep up with the running mice. *Where are all the spiders?* The mice were oblivious to the fact they were being followed and were desperately trying to get somewhere as fast as their little front paws and strong back legs would take them.

"I 'ope he doesn't see us late," said one of them.

"He'll kill us if he does," said the other.

What are they muttering about? thought Sid. *Who will kill them?* The mice arrived at the end of the long stretch of tunnel and vanished. Into thin air. Just gone. Sid's mandibles hung open.

"What?" he shouted. He hadn't realised that the mice had slid into a hole that he couldn't see from where he was on the roof of the tunnel, and he had to drop down to take a look. He couldn't see them anymore but heard them, and so he also jumped into the hole. What Sid couldn't see he was about to experience, as the mice had jumped into their quick entrance to the mouse hall, it was a corkscrew slide that took them from outside the kitchen into the cellar. Sid's legs whirled around his head as he tumbled and fell and twisted and turned as he corkscrewed down the slide. His spinnerets were shooting threads like crazy, but he couldn't get any purchase for his silk until he finally reached the bottom on his abdomen with all seven legs sticking straight up in the air. He looked like an umbrella that had been blown inside out by the wind.

He looked in front of him and saw a sight he would never have believed could exist!

"Oh no," said Sid.

CHAPTER 17

MOUSE HALL

In front of Sid was the biggest gathering of mice that he had ever seen. There must have been more than fifty scrambling and wrestling around each other. Squirming is a word you might have used. They were all trying to get a space, purchase on the damp cellar floor. It was a writhing mass of grey and brown fur with flashes of white as bellies were exposed.

Sid had fallen into a corner of the cellar that still had several boxes of items from when Lizzie and her family had moved into the new build. The mice had chewed through the base of the wall and then into the cardboard boxes to form an amphitheatre between the wall and the box on the other side. Box flaps had been bent over to form a platform wedged into the air by a picture frame fallen from the box. One of the other cartons had spilled old jumpers onto the floor, producing material for little snug nests all around the main stage of the platform. It looked like a mouse version of the Royal Albert Hall, with mouse nests instead of theatre boxes.

The nests were not held up by mouse structures though but by complex and intricately designed spider's webs. Sid now realised why King Rod wanted spiders in his army; he used them as building slaves. Rod himself was sat on the stage with a thin, scraggly mouse that Sid didn't know, but it was Whispering Wilf, the mouse who had captured Sid's sister. It was then that Sid saw the contraption on the stage. The contraption was a matchbox, and it was on its side. Matchsticks were set up like bars in a prison jail, and behind them was Sid's sister Jayne. She was alive but held captive by King Rod and his Guard Mice.

Sid very nearly shouted out to Jayne but at the last moment stopped himself. He did not fancy being chased by fifty mice. Instead, he backed into a corner behind the mice, who didn't know he was there, as they all faced King Rod who was giving a speech. Rod told how the spiders and mice lived together to protect each other and to create better lives for themselves, but Sid could only see one beneficiary from the partnership, and it certainly wasn't the spider race.

He looked closer at Mouse Hall, as he had heard Rod refer to this gathering place, and saw that every structure was supported by strands of web or silk. All the nests stuck around the sides were held in place by thick thread. The stage or platform that Rod was on was held up by cleverly constructed webs forming arches attached to the picture frame. Even the staircase to the stage was pieces of wood bound together by webs. The whole structure had been designed in such a way that any humans coming into the cellar would just see a pile of boxes in the corner without knowing what was beneath the bottom one furthest to the right: Mouse Hall, of course. Or as Sid thought it should have been called, Spider City!

Sid scuttled up the wall behind the mice. What did he do now? He knew where Jayne was but couldn't fight fifty mice. To be fair, he couldn't fight one mouse, let alone fifty! As he was gathering his thoughts, high up in a corner trying to look like a ball of dust in case a sharp-eyed mouse saw him, another spider came flying down the corkscrew slide and into the auditorium now known as Mouse Hall. He hadn't seen her for hours now, but Sid recognised Mad Harriet's bloated body immediately. Except H wasn't one to hide away from mice; after all, she had built many of the structures around her with her team of spider slaves.

Nearly half as big as the smallest mouse, she climbed up onto one of the mice at the back and started to body surf her way to the platform were Rod stood speaking. There were about half the mice in the main hall while the rest were in the woollen-made nests attached to the outside walls of the box and cellar wall. Rod saw Mad H approaching the stage. She had clearly had a change of plan as she now intended confronting Rod head on. With no Sid or Jayne as bargaining chips, what could she possibly have that Rod would need? If she didn't have something to barter, he would surely kill her dead where she stood.

She danced from mouse to mouse, stopping two rows back on the head of a baby mouse who wasn't going to cause Mad H any trouble. She shouted to the stage.

"King Rod. Any chance of my old job back?"

Rod was shocked.

"Where in the name of mousedom have you come from? It must be many seasons since I clapped eyes on you. And you've got fat."

"You've not lost much weight yourself, your highness. You look like a fat rat, not a slight field mouse anymore."

Rod's blood pink eyes flashed with anger, but no one moved. He calmed himself and spoke again. If he darted for her from the stage, she would be gone through some crack in an instant. Jayne watched, fascinated, from her matchbox jail and Sid also looked down on proceedings but, taking advantage of the turmoil below, had edged closer to the stage so if the chance made itself available, he could be down a thread and on the platform in a second.

Rod was perched higher in the air than Mad H and looked down on her as their conversation continued. For one second, he considered just leaping down and trying to catch her; after all, she had left him for dead.

As if reading his mind H said, "I know you think I left you for dead last time we were together, but you would have done the same. It was every creature for themselves. We just did what we had to do and look at us now, both here and still very much alive. So, it worked.

I also intended to bring you a gift to help get back into your good books, but you have half of it there in front of you, Jayne the spider, ready for breeding and adding to your slave army. Just let me run them again for you. I've heard you've been having one or two problems."

This was true; Rod had never really replaced Mad H, and a succession of mice and spiders had been tried in the overseer position but to no avail. There were still breakouts and uprisings no matter how many times the spiders were punished.

"Let me put this new one away and we'll talk," said Rod.

"I'll meet you in your throne room when you've finished with her," said H and then, shooting a thread into the dark heavens above, she scooted up and disappeared. Sid saw where she went, but he wasn't leaving Jayne. Now he'd found her, he was going to keep her in his sight, all eight eyes worth.

But Jayne was going into The Net with the rest of the spiders.

"Take her away," said Rod. "It's The Net for her."

The Net, thought Jayne, *what in the World Wide Web is The Net?*

CHAPTER 18

THE NET

The Net under any other name was quite simply a prison but something I'm sure you've never heard of before, a spider prison! No one knew for sure how many spiders were in there, but it must have been more than ten and less than a thousand. The final figure was certainly closer to a thousand. Rod thought more like a human than a mouse, and when he escaped that night from the fight under the shed and into The Edge, he decided he was going to be The King and do whatever it would take to be the King of the House.

He wondered what some of the human kings and queens of long ago may have done to remain on their thrones and decided he needed an army to help him build his kingdom. Where would he get an army in The Edge? There were no creatures behind the walls that had the skills to build the structures and designs that he had in mind. Who would be able to fulfil this task for him?

One day not long after he had entered The Edge and was still in the early stages of adapting from the garden to the house, he was sat below the boards of the kitchen floor. He was picking at small crumbs that had fallen through when something caught his eye, flashing in the weak winter's morning sun that feebly filtered through the cracks into The Edge. It was a large, fat spider making a web, but the web was catching the sun and reflecting into the pink beady eyes of soon-to-be King Rod, known at the time as Rod!

He watched the spider in the corner of the kitchen through a crack in the floorboards, squinting like a short-sighted man reading the eye test at the opticians. He was looking at Mad H but had never met her before so just saw a big spider doing what comes naturally to spiders, which was making an intricate, delicate-looking, orb-like structure that, whilst looking frail, was pound for pound as strong as industrial steel. He was transfixed. He would never have said this out loud, but Rod was watching nature as a thing of beauty as H flitted back and forth like a weaver at a loom and the magnificence of the web took shape.

Rod to this day doesn't remember exactly how the thought came to him, but the flashing of the sun through the web hypnotised him and then the 'Eureka' moment came.

That's it, he thought, *I'll build an empire with spiders. They will build for me and if they won't do it willingly, I'll make them.* From that moment onwards, he knew what he wanted and in Harriet, Mad H, found someone else who would do what was needed to survive well in The Edge. From these seeds of ideas came the spider slave army and the structures around The Edge that was literally held together by the threads, weaves, webs, and silks of hundreds of spiders used over the two years of Rod's reign as King Rod. And it was H's idea to design The Net as it was to keep the spider slaves under control. After all, who better to design a spider prison than a spider! H and Rod had an uneasy alliance right up to the point when she fled for her life into the garden, but The Net was very much her baby or spider sac, if you like.

Mad H found the tools available to make her prison in one of the boxes strewn in the corner of the cellar. The spiders, solitary creatures as they are, could not be coerced in any way or form to help the building of Rod's ideas of how he wanted his kingdom to take shape. So, he decided he would force them to help him under the threat of death, and then H came up with the concept of a prison. But how do you keep hundreds of small spiders trapped when, as we all know, they can get into the tiniest of holes and cracks?

H got some of Rod's Force Mice (called Force Mice because if they asked you to do something and you said no, they forced you to do it) to rip open the boxes to see if she could find some human item that would help her keep the spiders enclosed. What she found was several old net curtains. Old but not so old that they were torn or damaged, just old by human terms.

After several different and varied attempts, Rod and H eventually came up with a structure that would work as a spider prison. Draping the net curtains over three different size boxes and by dragging stones from the garden into the cellar as weights that held the edges of the net curtain down around the perimeter, they constructed The Net. It looked like a circus tent with three different height peaks. The cellar floor was concrete beneath the structure so there was no way out there. Force Mice patrolled the exterior with the one order that if they saw a spider trying to get under the net and escape, they must *eat it!* After a few failed attempts, the spiders stopped trying to escape. No one spider had ever escaped to live to tell the yarn.

There was one entrance and one exit to The Net, which was a triple flap of net held together with their own webs. Every time the mice released some spiders to build something or to open the flaps to imprison new captured spiders, they grabbed a large female spider to 'stitch' the entrance/exit up again. The spiders would then be marched to their place of work, guarded by Force Mice and marched back when they had finished. Anyone trying to escape was eaten. There were always plenty of other spiders to find and add to the slaves, and the female spiders regularly produced eggs, so the mice had no issue with numbers.

Sid watched his sister being thrown into The Net.

"Get in there and make some spiderlings," said the nasty Guard Mouse.

But Sid knew his sister, and it would only be a matter of time before she tried to escape. And please remember, every spider who had tried to escape had ended up as a mouse snack. Sid knew he had to help!

CHAPTER 19

NO ESCAPE

Sid watched as Jayne was taken by the Force Mice and marched through a maze of cardboard tunnels until they got to The Net. The entrance was opened for merely a second as Jayne was roughly thrown inside. Sid followed all this from high above, losing sight occasionally as some of the cardboard passageways had roofs and some were just corridors he could see into. At this point he was, watching from a stack of metal shelves that also housed several cardboard boxes.

Sid saw The Net and wondered at its three-peak structure. If it hadn't been built to trap spiders as slaves, he would have marvelled at the ingenuity of the mice. As it was, all he could think about was the danger his only sister was in and how in the name of the World Wide Web was he going to get her out safe and sound. He racked his tiny brain but could not come up with a plan that didn't involve great risk that would probably end with him being a mouse meal.

Meanwhile, Jayne was coming to terms with her new surroundings. Let me try and describe it to you. Once inside The Net, it wasn't a great open space but over the years had developed into a labyrinth of spider's webs and threads. It was a huge space, especially for a spider, but was filled with orb webs, circular webs, small rooms bordered by thick, layered threads and silks; literally, there were webs everywhere. There were many threads hanging down into a larger space in the middle of the web maze from which Jayne soon worked out that those on the outside had spiders descending and those towards the middle had spiders ascending. So, it was a little like a spider one-way system but up and down instead of left and right.

The strange thing to Jayne was that no one spoke to her. As we know, spiders tend to be solitary creatures, but they're not totally antisocial, and

Jayne thought someone would speak to her, but not only did no one initiate a conversation, no one answered her as she asked for help.

"Hello, can you tell me… excuse me, who's in charge here… am I supposed to go somewhere…?" Not a peep. Everyone seemed so busy and had somewhere to go or seemed to have something to do that no one stopped. Even if Jayne stepped into the path of an approaching spider, they just swerved out of her way and carried on as though she had been a hole in the road rather than another spider trying to engage in a conversation. Jayne would not have known what this word meant, and you may not know either, but the spiders had become institutionalised. What that means is that they had lived for so long under the rules of the spider prison that they thought that was the normal way of acting.

The spider slaves didn't know that spiders on the outside world would stop and talk to each other because in the prison they had been taught to mind their own business and get on with whatever the Guard Mice had told them they had to do. If they didn't do as they were told, they became a course on a mouse menu. Horrible, isn't it? But that's what slavery is all about.

Jayne stood in the middle of this never-ending melee of spiders like a traffic police officer directing traffic. Spiders sped around her, going in all different directions as well as scooting up and down the threads in the middle to get to other layers of The Net. She thought to herself, *how am I going to get out of here?* when a familiar face was thrown into the prison.

"You! You're the last spider I expected to see in here."

*

King Rod made sure that Jayne was safely delivered to The Net before making his way back to his own nest. Or, as he liked to call it, The Throne Room. It was a slightly grander than normal mouse nest. Room for six or seven mice rather than one. Layered with thick, warm wool from an old Christmas jumper found in one of the storage boxes, it glowed pleasantly with a red-green light. It was always Xmas in Rod's nest. Except, truth be known, it was never Xmas as, if ever there was a mouse with less goodwill to all men, mice, spiders, and any creature other than himself, it would be Rod.

Waiting for him, dangling from a thread just outside the entrance to his nest but high enough so she couldn't be grabbed, was Mad H.

"So, what do you have to say for yourself, Harriet?" asked Rod. "It had better be good or I'll never rest until you are gone. That is D E A D, gone!"

"I understand," replied the dangling spider. "I always knew it was a risk coming here today but one I thought worth taking when that spider offered me the job of guide."

"Who, that Jayne I've just thrown into The Net?"

"No not her. The other one. The one with seven legs. Sid."

"I have yet to make his acquaintance. That means meet him."

"I know what it means. Let's cut to the chase. I intended coming here today to patch up our relationship. We both know that I'm the best animal to run your team of spider slaves. I know I left under a cloud, but I swear that was never the plan. My spidery instincts kicked in, and I ran. I was going to bring you Sid and Jayne as an offering to your Net, but we never caught up with Jayne, and the last time I saw Sid he was sat on the back of a tortoiseshell cat, so that didn't go to plan. But who is your greatest enemy in the house? Not me but the black feline, and I have a plan to help you get rid of her."

"You mean Baggy. You think you can rid me of Baggy?"

"Listen up," said Mad H, "and I'll tell you how." And King Rod did listen and was extremely interested indeed!

CHAPTER 20

YOU ARE A WHAT?

Sid heard a noise at the back of the shelf and spun around faster than he could spin a web. In front of him, emerging from behind a set of bits for an electric drill, was a spider he had never seen before. The spider swaggered towards Sid, yes that's right swaggered, like an old western movie star before stopping just out of his reach. He then stood up on his two hindmost legs and thrust out his abdomen at Sid before he started singing:

"Manspider, Manspider,

Does whatever a man can do,

Builds a house, any size,

Catches mice, just like flies,

Look out.

Here comes the Manspider."

The spider then twirled around a bit, jumped up and down, shot a little thread before starting the second verse.

"Is he strong,

Listen chuck,

He has swallowed a full *Spiderman* book—"

"*Stop!*" yelled Sid. "What in the name of all things living are you doing?"

The spider replied, "I was singing to you. I'm Manspider. I'm a spider superhero. The humans have Spiderman, and the spiders have Manspider! That's me. I'm Manspider, but that's a bit of a mouthful so you can call me Peter." Manspider then stood again on his back two legs and expanded his chest. He had an unusual marking on his abdomen that did look like a slightly misshapen human capital letter M.

"Look," he said, "M for—"

"Manspider," Sid finished the sentence for him. "And what's that stuck to your head?"

"Nothing's stuck. That's my human hair when I turn into Manspider."

"No, it's not," said Sid. "It's cat hairs that you've stuck to your head with some silk."

"That doesn't matter; I'm here to save you all." And then, to the utter amazement of Sid the spider, Manspider – Peter, let's call him Peter – lifted the whole set of drill bits above his head. He followed this by shooting the thickest piece of thread Sid had ever seen completely across the whole width of the cellar, which was the width of the house.

"But that's impossible," exclaimed Sid.

"Not for Manspider," said Peter.

"Have you always been able to do this? Were you born this way?"

"Not at all. I have always eaten the correct foods and, if I say so myself, always looked after myself – that's what made me the man I am today."

Sid was in shock. "You think you're a man?"

"Don't be stupid," said Peter. "I'm Manspider."

Sid tried to compose himself. While it was obvious that this spider had immense strength and had silk the thickness of an iron nail that could shoot greater distances than should be possible, he wasn't exactly of sound mind. Slightly delusional. In other words, he made Mad Harriet seem like Sane Harriet! But couldn't he use someone like Peter to help him against the Force

Mice and King Rod? Which should lead to the freedom of Jayne.

"I need you to help me," said Sid, after thinking the situation through. "The mice have my only sister trapped in The Net."

"Why do you think I'm here?" replied Peter. "That's what superheroes do, help others less fortunate than themselves." Peter used a deep, affected American accented voice when saying this last part. "But let me tell you, I have only been Manspider for a couple of weeks. My powers come and go as I eat and go."

Sid asked the obvious question, "*What the hell are you talking about?*"

"Please let me tell you my tale that changed me from an ordinary house spider into a Manspider. About three weeks ago, I found myself in one of the rooms of the main house. Do you know the house well? I shall assume not. One of the rooms has many bookshelves, and on these bookshelves are not only books but things the humans call comics. There are hundreds of them. I was starving and hadn't caught a fly or bug for hours and so, in desperation, I decided to chew on one of the comics, not really to eat it, just to try it, see what it was like.

"Anyway, I swallowed a little, but it was horrible so I didn't try anymore until later that day when I started to feel really good; powerful is the word I would use, yes that's it – I started to feel powerful. I shoved whole, thick, big human books out of the way, and when I shot a small thread to drop down, it flew across the room. I didn't know why I was like this!

"So, for the rest of the day I practised and practised until I got the hang of my new powers. It was hard work, and I needed a rest so settled in the middle of my web for a doze, but before I did, I needed to poop. After I pooped, I felt really weak, well, not really weak, but in comparison to my power, I was back to normal. It was then that I realised I had pooped out the paper I had swallowed earlier. Forgetting about my nap, I scooted across to the 'comic' I had chewed on, and knock me over with a dandelion if it wasn't a comic called *The Amazing Spiderman*. I decided to eat some more and here I am today, Manspider."

Sid had sat down, not an easy thing for a seven-legged spider to do without a web. He simply didn't know what to believe.

"Let's get this straight. Because you swallowed some paper from a comic about a human superhero, who was a spider superhero, you became a spider superhero taking on the strength and power of a man. But only until you poop the paper back out?"

"That's about the size of it," said Peter.

Sid's mind was leaping ahead of him now. If this story were true, he would be able to help Jayne, and especially with Peter's help, but no one else must know. It had to be their secret.

Sid said, "No one else must know. It must be our secret. Did you try any other books or comics?"

"Just one," said Peter. "But it frightened me as I went missing for a day until I pooped."

"And what was that book called?" asked Sid.

"It was called *The Invisible Man*."

CHAPTER 21

WE HAVE EVERYTHING WE NEED!

"Peter, have you thought this through? You ate pages of a book called *The Invisible Man* and then 'went missing' for a day? I think what you mean is no one could see you! You were there but, as it says on the label, you were invisible. You didn't go missing; you just couldn't be seen."

Sid would swear to this day that he actually saw the lightbulb go on in Peter's head. Peter responded, "By the web of Shelob, you speak the truth. And there are so many books and comics up there."

"How do you fancy saving the lives of several

hundred spiders held captive by King Rod?" asked Sid.

Sid should have guessed the answer to his question.

"I am Manspider. Of course, I will save your friends." Peter stood up on his hind legs again, cat hair sticking in all directions on his head, and placed two legs/hands on his hips, looked out into the middle distance like all good superheroes do, while at the same time proudly displaying the M birthmark on the belly of his abdomen.

He might not be the brightest, thought Sid, *but he is certainly strong, and his threads, when shot from him, were like steel bars.*

"Can you take me to your books please, Manspider?" asked Sid.

"Follow me," said Peter and scuttled off to the back of the shelf.

*

Back in The Net, Jayne recognised Mad Harriet when she came into the prison. The last time Jayne had seen her, H was sat on her web at the bottom of the rhododendron. They had never spoken before, but H knew Jayne better as Sid's only sister. The spider she had been trying to get Sid to lead her to as a gift for King Rod was now stood in front of her as a prisoner in King Rod's prison. H was temporarily back in charge of the spider prison after she had sold her idea to Rod of how she would dispose of Baggy for him. The plan, as it was, needed the help of every single spider in The Net. H had decided to start with a carrot but then quickly move to a stick, an excessively big stick, if that's what was needed.

Jayne said, "You. You're the last spider I expected to see in here."

H responded, "Let me officially introduce myself. My name is Harriet; some spiders call me Mad Harriet or Mad H, but they only do it once to my face. You can call me Boss, but it's important you know what I do around here. I oversee the spider slave army for King Rod. Admittedly, I've only been back in the job for ten minutes after a several month gap, but nevertheless, *I am back*." I put that last bit in *italics* because Mad H *shouted* them.

Jayne never forgot her manners. "OK, pleased to meet you. Why are you talking to me?"

Mad H shared some of her plan with Jayne but not all of it. "King Rod has a nemesis, but as most creatures don't know what that means, including me, I shall say he has a number one enemy. That number one enemy, which you may or may not have come across, is a large black devil cat called Bagheera or Baggy to her friends. One of her friends I saw earlier today riding behind her ear, something that very few spiders, if any, ever get to do. That spider is a certain spider you know very well as he's not got the full complement of appendages."

Jayne looked puzzled.

"Oh, for the sake of Lolth. Your brother Sid Seven-Legs was seen riding behind the ear of Baggy the cat. King Rod and Baggy are the worst of enemies. Your brother knows the cat. Get your brother, which you will help us with, and we should know the whereabouts of the cat. Then we can get the spiders working, and we will get rid of old Baggy forever."

Jayne was overjoyed to hear of Sid. Up to now, she had no idea that he had been following her, and she took hope that all was not lost. If little Sid could overcome his fears and get to the house and befriend a creature such as a cat, there was still hope. Jayne scratched her head and asked, "But what happens to me and Sid, and all the other spiders, if we help you get rid of Baggy?"

H pondered before saying, "You will all be free to go and live your lives as you see fit."

Jayne might have been a lot younger than H, but she didn't believe one word of that last sentence, or if she did it was 'you' and nothing else. But if she could get to Sid, then between them both, they could work this out. She believed this as surely as if it had been written by the gods, but she knew not how they would do it.

"OK, what do you want me to do?"

H put a comforting arm (might have been a leg) around Jayne and said, "You, my new little friend, are going to be the bait in my spider's web." And with that, Mad H led Jayne back out of The Net in what was the shortest incarceration in spider history.

*

Peter led Sid to the bookshelves in the study of the ground floor of Lizzie's house. Lizzie's dad was a comic fanatic, especially superhero ones, and obviously an avid reader. There was *Batman*, *Superman*, *Justice League*, *Thor*, *Ironman*, *Green Lantern*, *Flash*, every superhero you could think of, including a couple of *Black Widows*. There was also *Beano*, *Dandy*, *Topper* and *Whizzer* and *Chips* from as far back as the 1950s. This was a real buff's collection. Plus, an extensive library of classics and modern literature, from *Moby Dick* to *Lord of the Rings*.

Sid looked at Peter and confirmed, "So, whatever you eat, you take on some of the characteristics of what's in the book or comic?"

"As far as I know," answered Manspider. "I've only tried one or two. I obviously liked *Spiderman* because I'm a spider. Sort of made sense?"

"Right," said Sid. "We have everything we need."

CHAPTER 22

BE CAREFUL WHAT YOU EAT!

Sid ate well from *The Invisible Man*. Manspider opened the book for him to page twenty, and Sid ate the first full sentence which read: 'On my right I saw one boy faint'.

"Are you sure I don't have to eat anything specific about becoming invisible?" Sid was concerned he may just faint, having read about fainting.

"No," replied Peter. "The magic is in the words of the whole book or the comic. It seems that whoever wrote the full story managed to include a little bit of magic in all the words. It's not one word or sentence but the mix of them all together that makes magic. And of course, the drawings in the comic books."

He's not as stupid as I initially thought, mused Sid. There's magic in stories and words, everyone knows that. Even humans know but so do creatures as well, including spiders, and thinking this, Sid munched away on the innocuous sentence. He started at the back; 'faint' soon vanished down his throat. 'Boy', 'one', 'saw', 'I' soon followed, and he started to feel a little sick. *Oh, this is coming back*, he thought. He spat some of the letters back out before he was sick, and they landed and spelled: 'I W aS Fai NT'.

As the letters landed, Manspider read them out loud and Sid started to fade, or you might even say he became fainter and fainter until there was no spider there to see.

Sid looked down at his own legs and could see all seven of them, but through the magic of words and books, Peter could see nothing. Sid Seven-Legs had become 'The Invisible Spider'. Sid sat down on the back end of his abdomen with a thump. To paraphrase a sentence from *The Invisible Man*, Peter said, "On my right I couldn't see one spider faint."

Sid shook his head to try and clear it. "Am I invisible?" he asked.

"Who said that?" asked Peter.

"I did," said Sid.

"Who did?" asked Peter.

"Me," said Sid.

"Who's me?" asked Peter.

"Sweet Lolth. This could go on forever. Do we have a shiny surface I can look at?"

"Is that you, Sid?"

Sid took matters into his own arms and legs and cast a thread over to the black screen of the TV hanging on the wall. He could see everything behind him but not himself. He wasn't there to the naked eye, but when he looked down at himself, he could still see his own body. He was truly invisible.

Swinging back to where Peter was talking to himself, he tapped the Manspider on one of his shoulders and listened to the scream that came from Peter.

"It's just me, Peter. Sid. This is what happened to you when you went missing. You turned invisible but didn't realise because you could still see yourself. It was just that no one else could see you, so you decided you went 'missing'. You were there all the time just invisible."

Peter responded, "This is really difficult to process, Sid. Let me feel you, then I know you are there." Peter stretched the arm parts of his legs out and felt the air in front of him.

"Ow, watch the eyes."

"Sorry! You are really there."

Sid said, "I'm invisible, and you have super strength and power. Between us, we should be able to cause all sorts of problems for the mice and free all the spiders. But before we go, I want a backup." Sid turned back to the bookshelf and was incredibly careful about what he chose next. Ripping part of a page, he attached it to himself, so it too disappeared.

I hope I don't have to use it, he thought, *but if I have to, I will.*

"OK, Peter or should I say, Manspider? This is what we are going to do."

*

Mad H had rounded up all her Guard Mice and Guard Spiders. Yes, there were some spiders who turned against their own kind just like H, and they formed a ring around the spiders from The Net as H walked them all to the site of her latest construction. This was going to be the one that brought Sid and then Baggy to her and King Rod and got rid of the cat forever.

The plan involved Jayne luring Sid, Sid luring Baggy, Baggy getting trapped and the rubbish collectors arriving on time. It needed intricate, delicate timing and a fair share of luck. This was the plan agreed with King Rod, and H knew her life depended on delivering it.

So, H and the guards, along with many of the Force Mice, corralled the spiders from The Net and marched them to the foot of the cellar stairs.

"OK, everyone, listen up." H was about to make a speech. After she finished, everyone knew why she was called Mad H. She addressed the spider slaves who had pushed Jayne to the front, not because she was their leader or anything like that but because if someone was to be killed, she was the last one in. The spiders had a strict 'last in, first out' principle when it came to surviving in The Net. Simply known as LIFO!

"I am going to give you all a simple choice today," started H. "You can do what I say and choose to live another day, or you can try to escape. This spider tried to escape on the walk here." A small, trembling male spider was led to the front. He lasted three seconds before a Force Mouse was licking his lips and burping loudly. Many spiders turned their eyes, eyes, eyes, eyes, away.

"I'm sorry I had to do that, but it won't stop me doing it again. Does everyone understand?" In their fear, nobody answered. H shouted, "I said does everyone understand?"

Over five hundred spiders nodded and said yes in union. Only Jayne showed any defiance and hurled the worst insult she could think of at Mad H, "You are like a *human*."

"Thank you," said H. "Here are the plans for the construction." Two Guard Mice held up a picture pulled from a magazine. It was a photograph of a large dam somewhere in America holding back a great body of water. It was the arched wall that H wanted the spiders to see.

"Half of the spiders are going to start to the left of the bottom step and half to the right. The Force Mice will divide you up. If any of you decide to run for it, you will be killed instantly, along with five of your co-workers, so not only will you be killing yourself but five of your friends. Do as I ask you, and you will be free to go at the end of the construction. Right, let's get going – we have two days to do this before the rubbish collectors come."

Back on top of the boxes, King Rod watched with interest. He should have got Mad H back months ago. She was the evillest creature he had ever known. She was crueller than he was himself but Good Lolth, she got results. He honestly believed he was going to be rid of that damned cat for good!

CHAPTER 23

"I'LL EXPLAIN EVERYTHING."

The spiders did as they were told. No one decided that today would be *The Great Escape*. They had two days' work ahead of them and after that, if they were still alive, they would be free to live it as they wished. That was according to Mad H, who spoke with the authority of King Rod behind her. The construction was nothing more than a giant web trap. There were to be seven or eight layers of web, the longest across the base of the bottom cellar step.

Then each layer, six inches away from the last, would be shorter in length but thicker in nature.

Several Force Mice took a cluster of spiders above the construction and commenced with building a large covering but in such a way that it was held by short, thin silks that could be cut quickly and the net would fall. The mice were forcing the spiders to build a giant trap that was being made to catch far more than flies for supper. Anything that walked or ran off the bottom step would be thrust into a sticky mass of web, the like of which had never been seen before. It was going to be so strong and thick, with four hundred spiders working on it, and then the net could be dropped from above, ensnaring whatever poor, unfortunate creature got themselves entangled.

Jayne could work out what she was making straight away. She was working on one of the first walls nearest to the step. Longer, and not as thick, it arched like the picture of the dam they had been shown. She knew what they were building: a trap, and compared to the size of a spider, a noticeably big one. The spiders slaved away, literally. The Guard and Force Mice patrolled up and down, and rest was hard to come by. Each section had a Guard Spider to ensure the construction was the shape and size required, while the mice simply snarled and made sure the spiders were too frightened to make a run for it but not too frightened to work. Not an easy combination, and every now and then, a spider would yell out in pain as a mouse administered punishment with a sharp bite for some perceived mistake or laziness exhibited by a spider.

The spiders worked for several hours, rested for thirty minutes when they were allowed to try and catch some bugs or other such food, before starting again. At the end of the working day, the first four walls of the trap had been built and most of the hanging cover held above the walls. The spiders walked wearily back to The Net now, too tired to do more than drag their aching legs. You could say they were all spun out!

Through the one door back into the prison of The Net, the spiders took themselves off to their own webs for a no eyelid sleep! Jayne, after working for more than twelve hours, had to make herself a web. Living life in The Edge was not turning out to be the experience she had expected. And where was Sid? She knew H was looking for him, but he was nowhere to be seen!

Jayne found a small section on the ground floor to the rear of The Net that hadn't been taken and started to spin her web. She was tired, but her spinnerets soon got going. She had to admit, it was very disheartening work after everything she had done in the day. Then, a small spider miracle happened. As she spun one side of her web and turned round, she saw that she had made more than she thought. *Don't remember making that bit*, she thought. Then it happened again.

She spun round and watched as her web started to form out of thin air. She was frightened – *am I going mad like H?* She stopped working completely and the web continued to form round her until it was totally complete.

"By Lolth, I've lost it," she said out loud.

"No, you haven't, sis," said a voice from the ether. "It's me, Sid. Please don't scream or shout. I'm here to rescue you."

Jayne's mandibles fell open as slack as an old, used web.

"Just go to the centre of your web for a sleep and stay quiet as you're starting to attract attention. I'll explain everything."

Dazed but obedient, as it was most certainly Sid's voice, Jayne did as Sid asked and moved to the centre of her web, her web in name only as Sid had built most of it.

"Now wait there," said Sid. "I just have something to do, then I'll be back." Sid invisibly scuttled away for a poop, so thank the spider Gods that he was invisible. Who wants to watch that?

Jayne felt the web move as he went away and then moments later move again as Sid made his way back to her, but this time, she could see a faint outline of his body as the magic began to wear off. It was disconcerting as she could see straight through him initially, but then his body started to fill in like a child colouring in a drawing book. And then there was Sid Seven-Legs. Three days after the crow had swooped away with his only sister, they were back together. Even if they were trapped in a spider slave prison held by a mad, cruel spider and a King mouse that thought he was a human!

Jayne and Sid hugged with all fifteen legs and arms wrapped around each other. Spiders can't cry because they don't have any tear ducts, but if they could have done, this would have been the moment.

"You have some explaining to do," said Jayne. "How did you do that trick? I couldn't see you and next thing I know, there you are, but I could see all the way through your body."

"No trick," replied Sid. "Just the magic of words."

"I have no idea what you are talking about. And while it is great to see you again, now we are both trapped in here."

"That's what you think, sis, but let me tell you all about it. As I said earlier, I'll explain everything."

And that's just what Sid did.

CHAPTER 24

INVISIBLE AGAIN

Sid told the full story to Jayne. Meeting H, getting to the house, the trouble with the toilet, meeting Baggy, following Jayne into The Edge, meeting Manspider and finally, what happened when you ate the words or ate the magic that's in words. Jayne was OK with most of the story but, even though she had seen it with her own pairs of eyes, found the last part of the story difficult to swallow. To which her hilarious brother replied, "You think that's hard to swallow, you should try and eat pages from a really old book like *The Invisible Man*."

Jayne then told her side of events. Starting with the crow, landing on the bed, meeting King Rod under the skirting board, going into The Edge, being held in the claws of Whispering Wilf, being thrown into The Net (explaining what The Net was), the spider slave army, meeting Mad H – definitely mad, confirmed Jayne – the plot to capture Baggy through Sid himself and then waiting for the rubbish collectors!

"So, what exactly have all the spiders been building?" asked Sid.

"A humungous trap of a series of walls getting thicker and thicker and as sticky as the spider slaves could make them and then a big one held up in the air ready to drop on Baggy, I guess?" Jayne explained as much as she could based on what H had shown her and what she had worked out herself as she had been working that day.

Sid continued, "Manspider is waiting out there for me. When you leave tomorrow with the other slaves to continue your work, I'm going to make myself invisible again and get out. What I need you to do is continue with King Rod and Mad H's plan for now and pretend you never saw me. Our hope lies in the element of surprise. You need to trust me, Jayne; I can get you out of here, free the spider slaves and save Baggy. Just trust me."

Jayne thought that she liked this new confidence her brother had acquired on his travels and went along with him. As we know only too well though, sometimes the best spun plans can be brushed away like a web with a feather duster. Jayne admired the confidence and his determination but still had an inkling that this may not turn out as they planned. And of course, as her and her brother got some well-earned rest and drifted away to spider dreamland, it turned out that she was right.

*

Hours later, Jayne awoke to find herself on her own again. Sid had gone. That was until she heard him whisper, "Don't be startled. I'm still here. I brought some magic words from *The Invisible Man* with me. I'll see you later. You might be lucky and see me too."

Jayne assumed that was her brother's attempt at being funny. He wasn't, funny that was, but she would sure miss him if he weren't there to try. The Guard Mice started to round up all the spiders and the entrance/exit was opened to march the spiders out again. They were, as it happened, ahead of schedule, but that didn't stop Mad H from getting everyone to the construction as quickly as possible. Finishing earlier than planned was a far better position to be in than being too late.

The work continued. As the spiders had been led out of The Net, Sid, silently, had slid himself out also and now was making his way to meet Peter the Manspider at the top of the cellar stairs, their pre-arranged meeting point. Sid knew what he was going to do: he was going to find Baggy and warn her about King Rod's plan to capture her and do something with her that involved the rubbish collectors. He didn't know Baggy that well but assumed she was more than a match for a few little mice, however big the mischief was.

What Sid was going to do was something that had been written about in the country of China over 2,500 years ago. According to many history books, a famous general called Sun Tzu was the first person to say never do what Sid was going to do. Sun Tzu, in an incredibly old book called *The Art of War*, wrote (and I've changed the words slightly so we can all understand), 'never underestimate your enemies'. But Sid was going to do that; he certainly wasn't the first and undoubtedly wouldn't be the last, but Sid's mistake would cost Baggy her freedom. Sid and Jayne did not know the full plan;

they only knew the parts of it that King Rod and Mad H wanted them to know. Sid was about to risk Baggy's life and he didn't even know it!

*

The construction had been completed. King Rod, with H and Whispering Wilf stood on either side of him, looked down from the midpoint of the cellar stairs.

"There's something quite beautiful about it," said Rod.

H puffed her abdomen out. "Told you I could get it done for you."

"Yes, you did, and you have, but we need to slot in the last piece of the jigsaw puzzle before Baggy arrives. I know we haven't seen that one's brother." He pointed a paw at Jayne as he said this. "But I'm sure he will be arriving with that black cat soon." He signalled to his strongest mice, along with hundreds of the spiders, and they started to pull on pre-constructed thick yarns. The last piece of the jigsaw rose, wobbling into the air. The mice guided it into position near the top of the stairs and then slowly lowered it down onto the third step.

King Rod wasn't quite sure what Lizzie called

it, but you and I would call it a skateboard. It was set in position ready for someone or something to come hurtling down the cellar steps. Something like a black cat perhaps.

Rod leaped down to where Jayne was being held and took her to the middle of the front wall, facing the stairs. Jayne was held with her back against the wall by two Force Mice as H spun a thick set of threads to hold her tight. Jayne struggled but to no avail. She was held tight and fast and could not move a leg.

"The final piece," said H. "Your brother will come flying through that door on the back of that darn cat, hit the wheeled contraption, shoot down the stairs and get flung into the web. We will drop the net from above and Baggy will be no more. A quick gagging and transfer to the bins, and before we know where we are, poof, no more Baggy." H laughed with a cackle.

King Rod came down next to her and said to Jayne, "And the first thing that wheeled board will hit is you. Nice knowing you, spider. The last thing you see will be your brother riding a cat with wheels just before you are splattered by it. Enjoy."

King Rod and Mad H turned and left to get prepared for the next part of their plan just as Jayne began to cry.

CHAPTER 25

CAT!

Invisible Sid and Manspider were hidden behind an old fridge on the opposite corner of the cellar to where Rod's box kingdom and The Net were located. When I say hidden, Sid wasn't because he had carried with him a piece of *The Invisible Man* and had eaten it to leave The Net without anyone knowing. Sid saw that Jayne had been taken, plus webbed and stuck to the front of the first wall of the trap. He didn't expect that. He also knew it was two days since he had sat on Baggy's back when Baggy had said she would look out for him down here every day. Well, that hadn't happened as a big black cat would stand out like a big black cat amongst a mischief of mice!

Sid told Manspider what he wanted him to do and left to search the rest of the house for Baggy. He did not see the skateboard being dropped into position as the last part of King Rod's trap, and his impatience would cost him dearly. Moving through The Edge, he went as fast as his seven legs would propel him. He was getting better at zooming around on his silks. One thing that Mad Harriet had taught him was the ability to trust the strength of his thread and in his own agility.

From behind the cavity walls, he looked around on the ground floor: kitchen – no; study – no; family room – no; living room – no; utility – no; where was the cat? While hanging from the living room ceiling, he saw through the window that Baggy was strutting across the front garden, looking for a place to lounge in the early morning summer sunshine. Lizzie's dad was out there as well, cutting the hedge. How could Sid get out there to warn Baggy about the trap?

He had forgotten he was invisible! Lizzie was watching something on the tellyvisual. He needed her to go into the garden or get Baggy into the living room. How could he do this? He realised if she could see him, he could frighten her out, but his invisibility was working against him for once. Lizzie couldn't see him to get frightened of him, and she was absorbed in a film about kids dressed up in fancy, old-fashioned clothes who burst into song every five minutes.

She couldn't take her eyes off it! So, what did Sid do? He lowered himself onto the tellyvisual and started to spin a web across the screen. Lizzie was watching the girls on screen dance; one of them was playing the daughter of a witch and had a cobwebby style dress on. At first, Lizzie thought it was a part of the dress, but then, as Sid worked harder and faster, this web took up the whole screen. Lizzie walked over to the screen and, in time to the music, let out a scream. She could see the web forming across the screen, but there was no spider making it. "Arggghhhhh!" *Where was it coming from?*

Lizzie ran for the living room door, nearly snatching it off its hinges, closely followed by the front door. As she started running, Sid attached himself to her retreating back and, hanging onto his thread, was pulled along in her wake, narrowly missing the edge of the door and the glass panels by the house entrance. Wasn't this an unbelievable few days? He had lived more in three days than he had in all of his previous months. He blinked his way onto the brightness of the lawn (at least he would have done so if he had any eyelids), deafened by the screams of Lizzie, "*Daaaaaad!*" she screamed, but Sid had already released himself from her back and landed on the lawn with a thump. Spinning webs around him, much like a spider parachute, helped him soften the blow and save his life. The commotion, though, had startled Baggy, who had immediately jumped and scutched up the fence, but again, not before Sid had attached himself to the fur on her tail. Sid was shouting for all he was worth, but it was such a little voice, especially with no visible body for it to come from! Baggy commenced to run along the top of the fence and invisible Sid flew up into the air again.

He was starting to feel like a waterskier who had lost control; well, he would have done if he had known what a waterskier was. Baggy trotted along the top of the fence, unknowingly pulling Sid from the front garden into the back garden. Sid still couldn't grab the cat's attention but was pulling himself along his own thread so he could at least get closer to the cat. Baggy then jumped from the top of the fence and landed on the lawn at the back of the house. Sid was catapulted into the air and his spinnerets worked overtime as he panicked, shooting threads for all he was worth in the hope that one would take traction.

One hit the fence but didn't stick. Another hit the wall but again wasn't enough of a direct hit to take purchase. He was falling and falling hard, but spider luck was on his side again as he landed in the fluffiest part of Baggy's tail! Finally, he could talk to the cat. Baggy had stopped and sat on her haunches as Sid climbed her body. Her giant tongue, giant to Sid anyway, tried to lick him off her body as he tickled her by climbing through her fur until he eventually got to her head and, swinging on a thread to her ear, yelled, "*Stop.*" Baggy stopped. Sid only had a little voice, but cats have superb hearing, and screaming into her ear, even with a tiny spider voice, was enough to startle her into freezing. "It's me Sid. And we have an emergency."

I don't know if you have ever seen a startled look on a cat's face, but if you haven't, quickly look at Baggy now. She is startled! I know you can't, but if you could, you would see a startled black cat.

"Now, don't worry," said Sid, "but I'm invisible."

CHAPTER 26

HOLD TIGHT!

"Being invisible don't matter none to me," lisped Baggy. "You spend most of your time with me sat behind my ear anyway, so I only feel you, not see you. But what do you mean invisible? None of us are invisible."

Sid answered as well as he could. "We have an emergency, Baggy. King Rod has…" No sooner did Sid say the mouse's name than the hackles went up on Baggy's neck, and she arched her back. She was fit enough to spit. Sid had to continue; he had no time for a drama queen moment. "King Rod, with the help of an old spider, Mad H, has captured a load of spider slaves." (Anything more than eight was a load to a spider.) "He has forced them to make a trap for you at the bottom of the stairs in the cellar. He's trying to get rid of you, and he has my sister held at the front of the trap, built from thick, thick silk by the way. I think they expect me to come and get you, and you will charge into it like a, like a, like a cat in a web." Sid had no concept of bulls in china shops!

"Well, they're correct. When I get hold of that rat, I'm going to tear him limb from limb."

"Rat?" questioned Sid.

"Rat," repeated Baggy. "You don't believe all that nonsense that he's a big mouse, do you? He's a little rat, the runt of the litter. He was ejected from his rat family because they thought he wouldn't live, so he's been passing himself off as a mouse ever since."

Sid could hardly believe what he was hearing, but then it started to make sense. No mouse would behave in the manner that Rod had, but rats, well, they're a much nastier kettle of fish. And when you look closely, he does have an exceedingly long snout for a mouse and his ears… all the lights go on at once in Sid's head!

"King Rod is a *rat*."

"At last," said Baggy, "you've got there. Not only a rat but a nasty one who thinks the only way to live is to crush others. He's had no love in his life and only wants to dominate. He's never had anyone to teach him how we behave in the animal kingdom and has learnt to live from human behaviour. That's where he will have got the idea of slaves from. Anyway, I'm going to separate his head from his body. Now I know where the trap is set for me, I can avoid it easily. Hold tight."

Baggy sprinted around the back of the house with Sid hanging on for all he was worth. He felt as though he'd been on every ride at the fun fair this morning, at least twice. All seven legs were buried deep in the thick fur on the back of Baggy's neck, but she was ignoring his pleas to slow down. This was exactly what Rat Rod wanted her to do. Baggy flew through the cat flap, slid across part of the kitchen floor, skidding in time to gain her feet and turn left. The door to the cellar was ajar.

Hitting the base of the door with a firm shoulder, Baggy burst through onto the cellar steps. She leapt into the air, missing the first two steps but landing clear as day on what should have been the third. Except it wasn't. It was a skateboard, and Baggy, with Sid on her back, went hurtling down the stairs straight for the trap at the bottom. The trap that had Sid's sister caught tight to the front. Sid was about to kill his one remaining sister.

"Nooooo," he cried as Baggy and the skateboard rattled down the cellar staircase.

*

While Sid had set off to find Baggy and bring her peacefully and quietly to the cellar, Manspider had his own part of Sid's plan to complete. Sid hadn't given Peter Manspider much to do; his task, should he care to take it, was to use his super strength and power to break out the rest of the spiders from The Net so that by the time Sid got back with Baggy, they would have the rest of the spider slave army to help them fight Rod and his Force Mice and Guard Mice and Guard Spiders, and not forgetting Mad H. So, that was all Manspider had to do. Luckily, he was as daft as a yard brush so didn't see any problem with this!

The very tired spiders were walking their way back to The Net under the watchful eyes of the Guard Spiders and Mice when Peter Manspider jumped out at the head of the trooping spiders.

"Stop right there." He held up one of his legs/arms in the internationally accepted symbol to stop. "I am Manspider, and I am here to save the day." Peter rocked back on his backmost legs and stood up, exposing the large M-shaped birthmark on his abdomen. There were audible sounds of approval from the slave spiders which mostly went along the lines of, "Ooh look at 'im." Two Guard Spiders tried to grab him but, like a western sharpshooter, he knocked them both flying with two bullet-like thick silks from his six shooter spinnerets. Again, audible oohs and ahs from his captured audience. Five more Guard Spiders tried to catch him but once more, *ping, ping, ping* – they were knocked into autumn, and it was only midsummer.

Two Guard Mice appeared. This would be the real test. One ran straight at Peter, aiming to literally chew him up and spit him out, but this wasn't Peter the spider; this was Manspider, who grabbed the top jaw and the bottom jaw of the Guard Mouse before wrapping the snout with a shot of silk. The Guard Mouse said, "Mmmmm mmmm," to the other mouse, who was quickly trussed and hanging in a collection of threads from the top of a watering can. Soon the mice were reunited and were both trussed and hanging. The whole tussle had taken no more than ten seconds. Manspider really was going to be a particularly useful ally.

"Right, spiders, you are going to have to fight for your lives. Now follow me, we're going back to save Jayne." And that's just what they tried to do!

CHAPTER 27

THE BINMEN

Manspider turned the slave spiders round, having strung up or detained all guards, four-legged or eight-legged, and was now marching a very weary army back to help Jayne and their oppressors. If you could have seen them, you would have witnessed the shackles of slaves dropping away like invisible weights from around their necks. Tired they may have been, but free spiders are a different animal to enslaved ones. Their passion for life came back as though Manspider had flicked a switch and the electricity had started to flow in each of the spiders' minds.

They started to run, especially the younger spiders. Then, several shot silks and threads and began to swing until there was a swell of feelgood, and the cluster of spiders became joyous at being free again. Not all of them scooted back towards the mice and King Rod; some scuttled away into the darkness, simply overjoyed not to be eaten by a rodent, but the majority stayed with Manspider, who had been overtaken at the front by many ex-slaves, but effectively, he still led the charge.

As Sid had given Manspider truly few instructions to work with, he simply said to them all, "Just cause as much chaos as you can. I have to save Sid's big sister. Don't put yourself in any danger if you don't have to, but let's keep these mice busy." Manspider saw the layers of the trap not far ahead of him now. Jayne was attached to the front as he expected her to be. King Rod and H had retreated to a position of safety high up on a shelf to watch proceedings unravel. Jayne was surrounded by Force Mice, who intended getting out the way should Rod's plan work.

Over four hundred spiders swung, ran, jumped, leapt, dropped and appeared, as if from nowhere, all at the same time. The mice were overrun. There were over twenty-five spiders to each mouse, and while a mouse can break out of a spider web with ease, it is a different story when there are twenty-five or more swarming all over you at the same time. Nipping, biting, tying their paws together with thick thread as several spiders combined at the same time to trip the mice up, attaching their tails to things so they were being pulled every which way, Manspider got exactly the chaos he was hoping for.

Manspider headed straight for Jayne, using his super strength to elbow any mice out of his way. He was like a rugby player – as the mice came diving at him from all directions, trying to make a tackle, he would hand them off or body swerve out from their reach.

King Rod could see this was not going to plan.

"Who is that spider throwing my Force Mice around like rag dolls?" he asked of no one in particular. Mad H wasn't about to answer as she had never seen a spider with such power in all of her life and was thinking it might be time to switch sides again.

Jayne looked across and saw the 'new' spider she had never seen before but who her brother had told her about. She wriggled to try and free herself as she saw her fellow spiders from The Net fighting to free themselves and to free her. *This is actually going to work*, she thought. But it was at that point that Sid and Baggy arrived!

Sid was screaming into the cat's ear.

"You must be careful. Don't just run in – that's what King Rod (although Sid was now thinking of the king as Rod the Rat) wants you to do. Hold back. Let's think a minute." It didn't matter what Sid said; Baggy was not for turning. She burst through the cellar door and landed on the skateboard.

Rod saw and cheered with glee. The skateboard rattled down the stairs, bouncing and careering its way at great speed towards Jayne. Jayne struggled to free herself from the web. Manspider was too far away; even with his power, he couldn't reach her in time. Baggy, without realising, had turned into a frightened cat, fur stood on end, back arched, grimace across her face – her claws had come out and dug into the wood of the skateboard, meaning even if she wanted to, she couldn't let go. Sid was holding on and looking into his sister's eyes as they drew closer and closer. The last thing that Jayne wouldn't see before she died was Sid, because he was invisible.

Baggy, Sid and the board bounced off the last step, and Jayne closed all eight of her eyes, except she couldn't because she didn't have eyelids, so she scrunched them up. Baggy screamed. Sid screamed. Jayne screamed. Manspider screamed and then shot one of his big, strong threads as sure as an arrow shot from a bow and, as the skateboard hit the first wall of the trap, Jayne was shot away by the thread of Manspider and landed stuck to the cellar wall. Still trapped, this time by Manspider's thread, but very much still alive.

That wasn't the end of the problem, though. The first web wall stopped the skateboard dead but not its cargo. Baggy flew headfirst into the rest of the webs.

"*Now!*" shouted Rod. The web that had been suspended in the air was now bitten through by the Force Mice stationed above the chaos that was unfurling below. Baggy tried to shout at the top of her feline voice, but her jaw was all stuck up with web, and the more she struggled and tried to scream, the more she got entangled and her jaw was stuck fast. She couldn't move or speak. She stopped struggling as she could only breathe through her nose and didn't want that to jam up or she would be a goner. Rod the Rat jumped down, landing on the top of his captured foe.

"Everyone, pull," he shouted, and the mice, who had forced the spiders to set up pulleys with their threads, did just that. Baggy swung up into the air; Rod guided the cat towards the big, black plastic bin that was going to be put out that very day for the Binmen. Baggy was dropped straight into the bin. Rod scrambled out and flipped the large green plastic lid shut. He ranted triumphantly, "We have her. Later today, Lizzie will push this outside, and Baggy will be taken. We will never see her again." H took her position next to her king.

Below him, the mice cheered. Jayne was still stuck to a wall, and the spiders had gone to wherever spiders go to when they're chased away in The Edge, Manspider with them. It looked like Rod and H had won, but where was Sid?

CHAPTER 28

THE INCREDIBLE SID

Sid was clinging onto the ear of Baggy as the skateboard careered its crazy way down the stairs. As the skateboard stuck in the first wall of web and Baggy flew into the rest, Sid was catapulted off Baggy and into the air, but don't forget, no one could see him – he was still invisible. He shot threads in every direction he could from his four spinnerets and, luckily for him, one took purchase on the wall directly ahead of him, and he scrambled up the silk to rest, panting, high up away from the action. From his vantage point, he watched as Baggy was parcelled up like a Christmas present and dropped into the plastic bin. Jayne was still stuck to the cellar outside wall.

Rod and all his mice were singing and prancing about. H was silent and watchful, suspecting that this conflict wouldn't be over until the fat spider sang. Manspider came from his hiding place. He decided that this was to be his moment. He could save Jayne and Baggy, which in turn would save all the other spiders. If Baggy left the house, then King Rod would rule The Edge forever, and that meant the spiders would become slaves again. Rod had said if the spider slaves did his bidding, they would be set free afterwards, but what he hadn't said was how *long* they would be free for! Rod and H fully intended recapturing their slave army once the Binmen had been.

Manspider dropped down from above on his thread, right in the middle of all the dancing mice. The mice stopped dancing. Rod faced up to the much smaller, but much stronger, Manspider, who rocked back on his legs, showing the M on his abdomen. Peter the Manspider wasted no time. He shot bullet-size threads from his spinnerets, this time looking every inch like a spider version of 'The Terminator'. Rod was ready. He had seen the power of this strange spider and had picked up two bottle tops as shields and was deflecting the thread bullets away from his body. Even when one or two got through his defences, he managed to deflect them away with his thickly muscled torso. After all, he was a rat amongst mice.

Manspider started to get frightened, and we all know what animals do when they get frightened. They poop! Manspider pooped. No one was aware because spider poop is so little you can't see it, but he pooped out the magic words from the *Spiderman* comic that had turned him into Manspider. His thread bullets got weaker and weaker until Rod didn't need his shields anymore and all that was being fired at him was slightly thicker silks than a normal spider would shoot. Manspider tested his strength by trying to push a mouse out of the way. The mouse didn't move. Manspider had gone; all that was stood in front of Rod now was Peter, an average-sized male spider for his age.

"Get him," said King Rod. "Whatever power he had has gone. Take him to The Net. He can be the first of our new slave army."

While all this had been happening, Sid took his chance. Running around the outside of the walls, he took himself to where Jayne was strung up. Whispering to her to stay still, Sid startled her all over again (it takes a long time to get used to your brother or sister being invisible; imagine the tricks you would get up to if it were you, and your sister couldn't see you). He loosened Manspider's thread enough to secrete Jayne away. It had taken him three days, but he had finally freed and saved his sister. Now was not a time to celebrate though, as Peter had been taken prisoner.

So, now Sid had to free Peter and Baggy. It seemed just as he got someone away from the clutches of King Rod and H, someone else went and got themselves caught! Plus, the invisibility was wearing off; after all, it had been a very exciting hour, especially on the skateboard. Sid had a secret weapon. He had taken paper from another comic. More magic words that hopefully would give him the power he needed to defeat Rod and H and free Baggy and Peter.

Sid said to Jayne, "I'm not sure exactly how this is going to work, sis, but I have to try something or Baggy's a goner. Lizzie will be down soon to do the bins, and once they're through the cellar door to the outside, I'm not sure how we save her." Sid took the paper from his pouch and scoffed it down through his mandibles.

At that very point, the cellar was flooded with artificial light. Lizzie was coming down to do the bins, and the floor of the cellar emptied as all the spiders, mice and one rat hid in The Edge or wherever they could. This was the moment. This was the moment when Rod won. If Lizzie pushed that wheelie bin outside, Baggy was away with the Binmen, the rubbish collectors! Lizzie banged down the stairs. This was a job she hated. She had in her hand a white plastic bag of rubbish that she had been given by her mum to put in the big bin.

Yes, thought Sid, *she has to open the bin. She'll see Baggy.*

No, thought Rod and H and all the mice, *she has to open the bin. She'll see Baggy.*

She walked to the bin that had Baggy trapped in it. Opening the lid with a sulky crash, she slammed it open and, without looking inside, dropped the white bag. It landed on Baggy with a soft umph but to no avail as Lizzie banged the lid shut without even looking inside. Lizzie turned the key to the outside door and pushed it open. She turned and grabbed the handle on the side of the bin, ready to pull it up the outside ramp.

Sid got angry. Then he turned green. Then he started to swell. His head and abdomen grew to twice the size. His legs popped out half as big again, except one that he didn't have. If spiders wore shirts, his would have ripped in half and fallen off his body. If spiders wore trousers, amazingly, these would have stretched an awful lot and stayed on. This was no longer Sid Seven-Legs. He had eaten pages from an *Incredible Hulk* comic and become 'The Incredible Sid' or, as he would forever be remembered, 'The Incredible Silk'!

CHAPTER 29

SHOWDOWN

Lizzie couldn't move the bin. It wasn't that heavy; it was just the general rubbish. They had several bins, and today was stuff they put into the metal bin in the kitchen. Not recycling. Not garden waste. Not plastic or cans. Not food. She actually wondered what went into this bin. Anyway, it wasn't heavy, but she couldn't move it. What was it stuck on? She went around to the other side of the bin as she was trying to pull it out the door, not push. What she saw would give her nightmares for weeks.

It was a *massive* spider, and it was bright green. And it was snarling! And it had teeth (mandibles to you and me) as big as a hedge cutter. (Not quite but you get the picture.)

Can you even imagine how loud Lizzie screamed? Lizzie didn't like spiders. But until that second, she didn't realise she absolutely *hated* giant green spiders. The Incredible Silk threw the bin across the cellar floor. The lid flew open. Rubbish tumbled onto the cellar concrete floor. Lizzie carried on screaming. Baggy fell out of the bin. Lizzie looked and saw what looked more like a mummified cat than Baggy. Lizzie carried on screaming.

The Incredible Silk came trampling from around the fallen bin. Lizzie screamed some more. She watched on through startled eyes as the green spider ripped off all the, what was it? It looked like web being ripped from the black cat wriggling like a giant silkworm on the cellar floor. Lizzie had a scream. King Rod, watching from the shadows of The Edge, raised a battle cry and led the charge to stop Baggy getting unwebbed. Lizzie tried to scream, but there was nothing left apart from a little croak.

Manspider and Jayne rallied around as many spiders as they could and raised their own battle cry. Manspider spoke, and the words came to him from a movie book he had nibbled on the bookshelf. He no longer had superpowers, but he remembered these words but changed them slightly for spiders.

"You've come to fight as free spiders and free spiders you are. What will you do with that freedom? Will you fight? Fight and you may die. Run and you'll live. At least for now. But you will die in your webs, many months from now. Would you be willing to trade all of this, from this day to that, for one chance, just one chance, to come back here and tell our enemies that they may take our lives, but they will never take our *freedom*!" Manspider had turned into Braveheart and all the spiders charged out onto the cellar floor to help save Baggy. Lizzie tried to scream but fell back in a dead faint instead. Her dad caught her as he'd just arrived at the bottom of the stairs and found it hard to comprehend what was going on in his own cellar. It was carnage!

Firstly, the big bin was strewn across the floor with coloured rubbish spilling out of it like the world's worst box of chocolates had been dropped. Baggy was squirming and wrestling, covered in some sort of net, scattering the rubbish even further around the cellar. But to top it all off, there were mice everywhere running around like it was a rodent adventure playground. Then there were spiders dropping from the ceiling in their hundreds like a war movie where all the soldiers abseil down on their ropes. Which is exactly what it was, except they were spider soldiers, and this was no movie.

Finally, sat in the middle of it was the biggest, meanest-looking spider Lizzie's dad had ever seen, except it was unlike any spider he had ever seen.

It. Was. Bright. Green!

Amongst the animals, there was the universal cry that it was time to get out of there.

"Humans!" Lizzie's dad held his comatose daughter and retreated back up the stairs, slamming the cellar door. A moment later, he was on the phone to the council pest removal.

The mice scattered. The spiders vanished. The Edge became full of spiders and mice. All except one spider and one mouse, except he wasn't a mouse – he was a rat. And once you knew he was a rat, you couldn't see anything else except a rat. The showdown was between King Rod the Rat and The Incredible Silk or, as you and I know him, Sid Seven-Legs.

Rod just saw a big spider and ran directly at The Incredible Silk. The fight lasted approximately three seconds. Rod just bit Sid's head clean off his body.

That's what would have happened had Sid not been The Incredible Silk, but he was and, picking Rod up with such force, he threw him into the sideways-facing bin. Rod hit the bottom with an almighty thump that knocked the bin backwards a couple of feet and completely knocked the rat out. The Incredible Silk flipped the bin upright again and, jumping fully three feet in the air, kicked the bin lid shut with one of his seven legs. Later, Lizzie's dad would tidy up and put the bin outside. King Rod would never be seen again.

As The Incredible Silk landed, the colour drained out of him, not a bad thing as that colour was green, and his body transformed back into that of Sid Seven-Legs.

Well, that was emotional, thought Sid.

CHAPTER 30

NEARLY THE END!

A couple of weeks later, everything was almost back to normal. Sid now had two homes: one in the garden, back in the rhododendron bush again, plus another web back in The Edge. It was obvious that Sid, Jayne, and Peter were held in very high esteem by the spider community at 2 Heath Bank, that was Lizzie's address in Lowcliffe where she lived near the sea. On the topic of Lizzie, she had some nightmares for a time to come, but she got over them. Kids are resilient.

The mice no longer had King Rod to lead them, so their bid for world power (house power) diminished. Baggy wasn't a happy cat when she was eventually sprung from the webs that had kept her still and silent at the bottom of the bin. She knew that Sid was her friend but would have trouble trusting a spider ever again. When Sid saw Baggy, he made it clear that it wasn't the spiders she should be concerned about but the mice and one particular rat.

After Lizzie's dad called the council, a man with more armour than a Stormtrooper turned up and laid poison traps all over the house. No good, though, as the mice all knew it was poison, but many of them made their way to new homes. Number 2 was a bit of a hotspot since the battle between the rat and The Incredible Silk. So, the mice made themselves scarce, and Lizzie and her dad soon forgot just how many mice and spiders they had seen that day.

Sid and Jayne had formed the spiders into more of a community. As we now know, spiders aren't that keen on company, but after the mice had managed to trap them all and turn them into a slave army, Sid and Jayne had weekly spider meetings under the rhododendron where the spiders could meet and have a social and just make sure everyone was OK. "It costs nothing to ask someone how they are," preached Sid. It was a lovely hot, late summer, with September being as hot as August before she was seen again. Yes, you know who I'm talking about. The one creature that had yet to reappear. Mad Harriet.

At one late summer meeting, a cluster of young spiderlings said they had seen something lurking about in the roses – it was a giant spider, they claimed. Peter, as he was not chewing down on books and comics every night and becoming a new personality, was now responsible for security. No one really appointed him; he just assumed the role, and no one argued, so he made sure his rover spiders kept their eight eyes open for anything strange.

A week later, a robin tweeted to Sid that she'd seen something strange under the garden shed. When the spiders investigated, there was nothing there. Jayne got back to her web one day to find it pulled apart. Whoever had done it was obviously angry about something. Other than these odd sightings, that Sid put down to the effects of the trauma in the cellar, everything went on as nature intended. Life was good again in the house, and Sid visited the house every few days now, but his home was the garden.

As the sun was dropping in late September, Sid and Jayne were saying goodnight by the back fence before they went off to their own webs. They were laughing and joking and generally full of the joys of nature. Jayne and Peter were getting close and there was talk of spiderlings.

"You'll be busy with a hundred babies to look after," said Sid. "Who will I be able to go on adventures with?"

"They'll have to look after themselves," said Jayne. "Back in our day, we never got special treatment. Anyway, Peter can do it. He loves spiderlings." They both laughed, shouted goodnight and went in opposite directions to their own webs.

Just as Sid got to his web, two branches down on the left, by the apples now as he'd moved up in the world, or was that down? He heard a noise. What was that? *Probably an owl*, he thought. *I've seen one flying about.* He moved across to the middle of his web, ready to not shut his eyes, when from underneath him, a claw shot upwards. It wrapped around his body and pulled him down onto his own web. A hot, salty breath oozed into his face, making him flinch.

"Got you," said Mad H and, holding one claw over his mouth, she slowly started to wrap Sid up in her silk!

EPILOGUE

(THAT MEANS NEARLY THE END BUT ACTUALLY IS THE END!)

Meanwhile, in Colombia, a tarantula spider called Isabella had got some news through the World Wide Web. Her cousin twenty-seven times removed had got into trouble. She had to go and help. She had fallen in love with his photo on FaceWeb and had to find him. She lived close by to the banana packing plant in the outskirts of Bogota and knew what she had to do.

She waited for the night shift to finish packing the latest consignment of freshly picked bananas.

Lowering herself gently down from the roof girders, she looked through all the boxes until she saw the one she had to jump into. (I've made this sound quick, but it took her most of the night as there were over two thousand boxes of bananas. And one banana looks just like another.)

Reading from the side of the box, Isabella said, "Lidl, Lowcliffe, Dorset, England. That's where I need to go to help my troubled cousins."

Climbing in, she crept behind a juicy bunch and, after making a web, went straight to sleep.

The next day, the bananas, with Isabella, were loaded onto a cargo plane to Bournemouth Airport. She was on her way to help her cousin. And guess what his name was… correct – Sid Seven-Legs!